W0232974

ROSES ARE BLOOD RED

Novoneel Chakraborty is the bestselling author of fourteen bestselling thriller novels and one short story collection titled *Cheaters*. His novel, *Forget Me Not, Stranger*, debuted as the No. 1 bestseller across India. While *All Yours, Stranger* ranked in the top five thriller novels on Amazon, India—the only one to feature amid other international bestsellers. His novel *Black Suits You* was in top five thrillers category on Amazon for fifteen weeks. While his Forever series was in the bestseller list for ten weeks straight after its release with *Forever Is A Lie* featuring in the highest selling books on Flipkart for 2017. *Forever Is True* made it to Amazon's Memorable Books of 2017 and *Times of India*'s Most Stunning Books of 2017.

Known for his twists, dark plots and strong female protagonists, Novoneel Chakraborty is also called the Sidney Sheldon of India by his readers. His immensely popular thriller series, The Stranger Trilogy, has been translated into six Indian languages and has been adapted into a popular web series, titled *Hello Mini*, on MX Player produced by Applause Entertainment and Rose Movies. His erotic thriller novel, *Black Suits You*, has been adapted into the blockbuster hit, *Bekaaboo*, while his exclusive digital novella, *Red Suits You*, is also being adapted into a web series by Alt Balaji. His short story collection, *Cheaters*, is now available in Hindi as well.

Apart from novels, Novoneel has written and developed several TV and web shows for premiere channels and platforms. He lives and works in Mumbai.

ALSO BY THE AUTHOR

Half Torn Hearts
The Best Couple Ever
Cheaters

FOREVER SERIES
Forever Is A Lie
Forever Is True
Black Suits You

THE STRANGER TRILOGY
Marry Me Stranger
All Yours Stranger
Forget Me Not Stranger

EX
How About A Sin Tonight?

ROSES
ARE
BLOOD
RED

Even True Love Has A Dangerous Side

NOVONEEL CHAKRABORTY

Penguin
metro reads

An imprint of Penguin Random House

PENGUIN METRO READS

USA | Canada | UK | Ireland | Australia
New Zealand | India | South Africa | China | Singapore

Penguin Metro Reads is part of the Penguin Random House group of companies
whose addresses can be found at global.penguinrandomhouse.com

Published by Penguin Random House India Pvt. Ltd
4th Floor, Capital Tower 1, MG Road,
Gurugram 122 002, Haryana, India

Penguin
Random House
India

First published in Penguin Metro Reads by Penguin Random House India 2019

ISBN 9780143449508

Typeset in Requiem Text by Manipal Technologies Limited, Manipal

Printed at Repro India Limited

www.penguin.co.in

MIX
Paper from
responsible sources
FSC® C047271

For my opening and closing brackets

Prologue

It was an important day for her. *Very important.* He was coming down to meet her after . . . in fact, she had been counting: three months, fifteen days, eleven hours and—as she left her house—exactly nine minutes. She had told her parents that she would stay with her bestie from college—Pragya—that night. Pragya, obviously, had no idea about her subterfuge.

He had selected the venue for their clandestine meet. It was only two blocks from her house to the small tea shop that would have closed for the day by then.

Despite the several layers she had on, Aarisha's teeth chattered as she cycled towards the tea shop. The shiver was partially due to the unseasonal cold wave that had gripped the Himalayan town; she trembled more in anticipation of the impending rendezvous. *Should I launch into his arms as soon as we meet? Or should I stand back and simply admire him for a bit?* With an avalanche of thoughts crashing through her mind, she finally reached the location for their tryst. She stopped her cycle as soon as she saw the silhouette of a man in the blinding headlight beams of the car parked in front of the tea shop. *He's here!* Her lips went dry, her throat, drier, and a flock of butterflies invaded her tummy. He had always been unpredictable.

The car's engine was abruptly switched off, simultaneously killing the headlights and plunging the deserted lane into a darkness which was underpinned by an eerie silence. Aarisha could still make out his blurred outline as her eyes adjusted to the dark. He was waiting for her. She hurriedly dismounted from her bicycle and let it crash on its side on the tarmac. She ran to him and embraced him. He could feel her pulse racing and her heart pounding in her slim body as she held him close and burrowed her face against his chest. He realized that she had missed him badly. He had missed her too, way more than she could ever imagine, but he didn't show it. Aarisha felt his strong and steady heartbeat against her face. He held her close to his chest for a moment before he scooped her up in his arms and carried her into the car. No words were spoken as he sped off down the lane. After driving for ten minutes or so along the winding mountain road, he pulled into a soft shoulder. The narrow mountain road was flanked by the steep rise of the mountain face on one side and a sheer drop on the other. He reached under the seat and adjusted the incline of his seat to a comfortable angle. Aarisha moved across to straddle his lean hips. Their eyes locked and she leaned forward until she could feel his breath tickle her chin. He was so much about silence—it drew her like nothing else. Most couples chatter nineteen-to-the-dozen. Only the rarest find their harmony in silence. They were rare, she knew.

She cupped his jaw in her long-fingered hands and caressed his three-day-old stubble with her thumbs. He stretched out an arm to flick the switch on the car stereo. Ariana Grande's husky voice softly permeated the interior of the car with one of her favourite tracks: 'God is a Woman'. Aarisha leaned in, but before their lips could touch, he gripped her waist and stopped her descent.

'Not so quick, Ranisa,' he whispered.

She loved it when he called her by that name. 'Ranisa' meant queen—*his* queen. If there was one thing she absolutely loved and couldn't quite define, it was his enormous respect for her. It was so deep-seated that she often wondered whether she deserved to be placed on such a high pedestal.

'You always say this,' she whispered petulantly. 'Don't you want to kiss me?'

He stared at her beauty, her dark hair cascading like a cloud around her shoulders. Her eyes didn't reflect pain, they carried a complaint.

'D'you honestly believe that I don't want to kiss you?' he asked.

'Then why don't you?' she sulked. 'Also,' she dismounted from him and scrambled back into her seat, 'I hate it when you leave me and go away.' He sensed the flood of tears about to burst through the dam at any moment.

'Why?' he asked softly.

'I feel insecure about you, about us,' Aarisha choked.

An ironical smile touched his face. 'You know this thing we call *love*, it's like a dense forest. As you enter, you hear the growl of several wild beasts. At times, you may even encounter them. Insecurity is the most ferocious beast in this jungle. Whether to fall victim to it or vanquish it to continue one's quest to unearth the greatest treasure ever, which is also hidden in this very forest, is the lover's call. I've taken mine. What's your call, Ranisa?'

She stared at him, amazed at the total conviction in his eyes. *How could someone's eyes always reflect such confidence?* It was the kind of assurance one developed after scrutinizing life so closely that its tricks became only too predictable. She leaned over and kissed his closed eyelids.

'I'll fight. I promise I'll fight all the beasts that come our way,' she whispered.

There was a faint smile on his face as he said, 'Don't worry about the distance between us.' He raised her downcast face and kissed her forehead, 'The body is only what *is*. The soul is what *is*, what *was* and what *will be*. The scope of all the urges stemming from the body is a mere molecule compared to the intense longing that arises from the soul. And for the soul, distance is an alien concept. Distance only restricts the body.'

'But the body is also important in its own way, isn't it?'

'As much as a house of bricks and mortar, because it houses the vulnerable and the fragile within. But we all know that the shelter is temporary and, as all temporary things, too transient to worry about.'

'What's permanent then?' Aarisha asked.

He placed his right hand flat against her left hand, palm to palm, their fingertips splayed until they found the gaps through which the fingers slipped, and the hands clasped each other.

'This,' he said, tightening the clasp, 'this is permanent.'

I wish I could tell you the number of wars I've fought to make this permanent, he thought.

'D'you know, there are times in your absence when I get the feeling that I hardly know you at all. Is that good?' she asked, resting her head on his shoulder.

'You'll know. You'll know very soon. It's just a matter of one more year.'

'One more year?' she asked, frowning.

'Yes. In one more year I'll gift you a love story that every girl desires, but few, if any, get to live,' he whispered.

'What do you mean?' she drew back to look at his face. There was no response. She raised her head—and suddenly she felt a tug on her hair.

'Ouch!' she yelled. Before she realized what was happening, she felt a punch on her face that broke her nose and lacerated her lips. The second punch that buried itself in her gut almost made her throw up. Aarisha fell unconscious, her face a bloodied mess. Three more punches followed: one to her jaw, another landed in her ribs and the third, in the stomach again. He shoved her away from him with force. The side of her head slammed against the window. He yanked down her jeans, slipped them off her legs and tossed them out of the window. He tugged her panties down to her knees and from his pocket he extracted a vial of semen. He smeared some of the semen on her panties, on her dress and emptied the rest on her bare abdomen. He made sure nobody would ever track down whose semen it was. For a doctor, it wasn't even a task. He dressed her back in a hasty manner.

As soon as he was done, he used his cell phone to call the local police station. Emotionlessly, he relayed the information, 'A girl has been raped and abandoned on the road.' He gave them the approximate location before hanging up. He glanced at Aarisha's unconscious battered face and muttered, 'The first thing you should know about me is: I . . . Don't . . . Let . . . Go . . .'

He turned on the ignition, opened the passenger side door and pushed the girl's insensate body out. He put the car into gear, gunned the engine and sped away into the night. After half an hour of driving, he stopped. He alighted from the car and stood at the edge of the abyss, gazing into the darkness. He dialled the police again. They informed him that the girl had been rescued and countered with their own questions about his identity. In reply, he flung the phone into the abyss as far as it would go. He looked up at the night sky— at the constellations of stars—they had mocked him enough. They thought she would never be his. And now, he would win her from everything—and everyone.

He extended both his middle fingers skywards and bellowed a bloodcurdling war-cry against destiny.

Vanav Thakur was no ordinary man. He was soul-deep in love with a girl. And he was a man with a plan.

BOOK I
THE PRESENT

1

The third house, a little away from the perennially busy Gaffar Market in Karol Bagh, always buzzed with one thing during the day: Binny Bagga's ear-splitting voice. She had the special talent of shouting at everyone—from her eight-year-old daughter, Sirat Bagga, to her husband, Anurag Bagga, who ran his own mobile phone store in Palika Bazaar. Even her widowed mother-in-law, Yashodhara Bagga, wasn't spared her scolding. The household, like one of those relentless prime-time soap operas, would incessantly generate reasons for Binny to bring the roof down by yelling at someone. Today, it was the impending arrival of a guest while the house looked like it had been hit by a tornado. If it were just any guest, Binny wouldn't have cared too much. But this was her childhood best friend coming over for lunch—and they were meeting for the first time after a decade although they had sporadically kept in telephone contact. The perils of adulting, she always told herself, whereby one starts believing that one's immediate priorities are the only important things in life.

Between tidying the house and preparing her best friend's favourite *chole chawal* (chickpeas and rice), she went to the salon for two hours. It surprised her husband, Anurag. The last time she had spent so much time in the salon was just before going for their honeymoon.

'Are you sure he's only a "best friend"?' asked Anurag. He was brunching that day so he could keep his shop open all day without having to break for lunch.

'No. He's actually my husband. D'you have a problem with that?' Binny snapped at him spitefully. Anurag understood that it was one of those days when his wisecracks weren't welcome. After his meal, he quietly left the house, climbed into his Alto and drove off. Binny helped her mother-in-law with her lunch, picked up Sirat from school and fed her before putting her down for her siesta and then waited, glancing at the clock impatiently. He had said he would be here by 2.30 p.m. and she was aware of his pernickety punctiliousness for punctuality.

The doorbell rang precisely at 2.30 p.m. Binny hurried to the door and opened it. The vision she beheld on her doorstep took her breath away. It was a man in full military regalia. He tucked his cap under his left arm, saluted smartly and said, 'Captain Dr Vanav Singh Thakur reporting, ma'am.'

Binny flung herself at him and gave him a tight bear hug. 'You've no idea how much I've missed you,' she choked. An acquaintance of the truculent and tough-as-nails Binny of the Bagga house would have been hard pressed to recognize this emotional clinging woman.

'I know. I'm sorry I couldn't meet with you before now,' he caressed her hair.

4

'Before now?' she reared back to glare at his face. 'Do you realize, it has been ten whole years?' She buried her face in his shoulder. 'You know I love you, right?' she whispered.

'I know. I can hardly believe it,' he whispered back.

She looked up, saw his amused expression and broke the embrace, 'You don't believe it because you're a *kutta* (dog)!'

'Won't you ever grow up?' Vanav chuckled.

'For you . . . never! Come on in,' Binny yanked him into the house and shut the door behind him.

'Put these somewhere,' Vanav handed her a large bag of gifts for her family.

'Why are you so formal?'

'Bringing something for the people one cares for isn't a formality. Where's Anurag?'

'He has gone to work. He wanted to meet you but . . .'

'That's okay. Next time, perhaps.'

'It's more than okay. I get to spend time just with you.'

'And where's the little princess?'

'Fast asleep now. She is my only blessing.'

Vanav's parents had told him how late a pregnancy Binny had underwent and with what difficulties. He was happy it was all worth it.

"You must be starving. Let's have lunch first.'

The chole chawal was one of the best he had ever had. It was followed by *faluda* (a milk-based Indian dessert). This was the first time in years that he had broken from his strict food regime.

While they lingered over dessert, Sirat woke up. 'Who are you?' she asked from the door of the dining room.

Binny pre-empted Vanav, 'He's your daddy as well.'

Vanav scowled at Binny before scooping up Sirat into his lap, 'Call me *chacha* (paternal uncle).'

'That's good,' said Binny, sotto voce, 'if you'd said *mama* (maternal uncle) I would've punched your nose.'

Vanav gave her a you're-incorrigible glance. Sirat smiled as Vanav kissed her cheek.

'*Beta*, go to *daadi* (grandma) now,' Binny gently took Sirat from Vanav and nudged her to the door. 'Let's go to the terrace,' she said to Vanav as soon as the little girl scampered out.

They gazed out at the view of the frantic activities in Gaffar Market from the terrace. Vanav said, 'This is all so strange. I find it hard to believe that you're all grown up and a mother to boot.'

'What do you mean?'

He immediately apologized. 'I'm sorry. I meant you and I were a couple of toddlers and look at us now, you're managing an entire household.'

'A household full of strangers,' Binny said.

He noticed that Binny hadn't lost her acerbic humour.

'How are things with Anurag?' he asked.

'Good. I don't know about him, but I'm certainly looking for a boyfriend.'

'Come on!'

'Why? Don't we all need some excitement to break the monotony of our humdrum lives?'

'Not everybody. That's applicable to only the few who never really knew what they wanted in the first place.'

Binny narrowed her eyes, unconvinced, so Vanav expanded on his theme, 'There's something called "fake hunger". It's when the body doesn't actually need food, but the fake hunger pangs make you crave food. Similarly, fake wants of the mind also exist. They happen so that we can stumble across what we really want . . . if we're lucky.'

'Whatever. Forget it. What else is going on? How are uncle and aunty?'

'They're good.'

'Don't they pester you to get married? I'm so looking forward to your wedding,' Binny said with an evil grin.

'Why?'

'Then we'll raise a toast as we'll be in the same sinking boat.'

'Isn't marriage beautiful?'

'I think the coming together of two individuals in love is beautiful. So, if one is married to someone whom one genuinely loves, then it is, I guess. Otherwise it's merely a lot of pretence on an everyday basis. Marriage entails a lot of duties as well, so, we make a choice between love and duties, forfeiting one for the other. Some stick it out because of love and some, like me, sustain it for the duty part.' Binny's gaze alternated between the bustling view and Vanav's face as she spoke.

'You have a caring husband, a lovely kid and a fairly good social position. Aren't you happy, Binny?'

Binny took a deep breath, 'I don't have the one I always wanted.' After a lingering look into his eyes, she looked away, 'So, am I happy? Yes, yes, I am. At least that's what I tell myself every morning before I begin the day. Sometimes make-believe is a boon.'

'I'm sorry, Binny.' Vanav turned away to look into the distance, at nothing in particular, 'I know I've broken your heart. I do know what it is to have a broken heart, but I still had to do it.'

'I know you didn't do it intentionally. If she hadn't happened, I'm sure we would have been a married couple by now.'

'Perhaps. But I guess it was inevitable that she had to happen. Just like growing up is inevitable. However, I do wonder at times: what if she hadn't come into my life? How would I have turned out? And then I feel I know the answer: she had to happen for me to become this version of me. Even if we weren't meant to be with each other, I was certainly made for her.'

Binny glanced at his handsome profile. How could someone be in love with an absent person for this long? People generally got tired of someone's constant presence. But here he was, a person who loved a woman for so many years without having been in touch with the object of his love. If that wasn't absurd, Binny didn't know what was.

'I just don't understand your love for her.'

'I don't understand a lot of things as well. I've stopped thinking about them,' he turned around smiling.

'Won't you ever get married, Vanav? Will you always be in love with her absence? Doesn't the loneliness bother you at all? And what about your sexual needs?'

Vanav gave her a sharp glance and said, 'I'll just pretend that I didn't hear that last bit.' He looked into the distance and sighed, 'That's the thing. I never get tired of her. Of my love for her. Of her absence,' he looked at Binny's uncomprehending expression. 'This thing called absence also becomes a kind of presence over time. In fact, if love was only about loving a person who is physically present for you, then I don't think love can even be a worthwhile emotional adventure.'

Binny couldn't help be amazed at this insight. Somewhere, deep in the recesses of her mind, his absence had also become a presence within her.

'And by the way,' he turned to her, 'who said I'm single?'

Binny raised her eyebrows, 'Okay . . . finally, you're talking turkey.'

Vanav smirked.

'So, who's the girl?'

'Aarisha, who else,' Vanav smiled charmingly.

Binny's curiosity popped like a bubble, vaporizing in an instant. Binny had always prayed for a miracle for her best-friend-cum-first-love. If not for a miracle, there was no way Vanav could have ever won Aarisha Shergill.

Only Vanav knew how he had made the impossible possible.

2

TOSH, HIMACHAL PRADESH

The thin mist suspended in the chilly air seemed to deaden sound, engulfing everything in a spooky silence. Vanav emerged from the foggy mantle of darkness like a figment of someone's lucid dream.

He headed to the cottage where a gleaming name plate read: Shergills. He opened the gate cautiously, taking care not to make any unnecessary noise as he stepped into the premises. Dude, the golden retriever he had bought as a puppy for her, now fully grown, came running over, wagging its plume-like tail. It licked his shoe. Vanav knelt and patted the dog's beautiful head before making his way to the front door.

The main door was kept unlocked as usual for whenever he was due to visit. Stepping inside, he locked the door from inside and walked over to the dining table. He dumped his bag on the sideboard and then went up to the second floor to Aarisha's room with Dude still at his heels.

In the light of the table lamp that was still on, Vanav could see that she was asleep on the bed, a book on her bosom, her spectacles askew on her nose and her lips, parted. Her phone was getting charged on the bedside table. He picked up the book and placed it on the table, careful to mark the page that she had been reading with the cardboard bookmark. He gently removed her spectacles, folded them and put them on top of the book. He sat down beside her to admire her beauty. *If ever a dream had a face*, he thought, *this was it*.

He loved gazing at her when she was oblivious of his presence. It wasn't solely to appreciate her beauty; he did this to convince himself that everything had gone according to plan. He was deeply grateful that it did. He bent close to her open mouth and inhaled the air she exhaled. A profound relief came over him and he stood up. He had reached for the switch of the table lamp to turn it off, when he noticed the note stuck on her cork bulletin board. It read:

Dear Mr Boyfriend,

I'm told you smoke a lot. One cigarette, they say, reduces five minutes of your life. How about every time you feel the urge to smoke, you think about me instead? I don't take life.

Vanav smiled, peeled off a fresh post-it from the little pad on her study table and wrote:

Dear Ranisa,

Your wish, my destiny. BTW, I've restocked your medicine cabinet with medical supplies including sanitary napkins; the fridge with your favourite beer and macaroons.

He pasted it right beside her note, peeled off another slip and wrote:

> *This isn't merely a nose stud; it's part of a story—your story, my story—our story. Wear it tomorrow and meet me by the Tosh river. It's a date, Ranisa.*

From his pocket, Vanav extracted a small box containing an exquisite jewel embedded in a tiny nose stud and put it on the study table with the post-it pasted across it. He covered her with the thick duvet lying at the foot of her bed and switched off the table lamp. Before turning away to leave, he kissed her forehead fleetingly. This touch was what he had craved for. It wasn't merely a touch; it was life whispering to his soul.

An hour later, Aarisha awoke with a start. One glance around and she knew someone had been there. She didn't need to guess the intruder's identity. Aarisha clambered out of bed and ran into the balcony. Despite the night, shrouded in silence and misty darkness, she sensed his presence. Her heart told her he was lurking somewhere at the edge of the darkness.

'Vanav Thakur, I love you,' she called. Nothing stirred, so she returned to the warmth of her room.

At some distance from the house, a flame from a lighter lit up a part of his face. Vanav pulled out his box of cigarettes and set fire to the entire packet, cigarettes and all.

'I love you too, Ranisa,' he murmured. Vanav vanished into the mist as if he were never there.

Aarisha retrieved her book and glasses from the bedside table and carried them over to her study table, pulling a face. *Why doesn't he let me know when he comes over to visit? Why is it so hush-hush?* At the table, she noticed something and switched on the lamp. A smile appeared on her face as she read his note. She opened the little jewel box, gasping at the beautiful ornament. She re-read the note about the date night. Every word in the note escalated her excitement.

'This man!' She blushed. *How did I get so damn lucky?*

3

'Fuck, fuck, fuck!' Aarisha hollered at the mirror. Her long-suffering bestie, Pragya, sat on the bed smiling wearily. It had taken two whole hours for Aarisha to approve the dress, the make-up and hairstyle for her date tonight. And just when Pragya was heaving a sigh of relief, Aarisha decided that she looked terrible.

'Even this looks terrible.'

'Why are you being such a drama queen?' Pragya asked. 'You look perfect.'

Aarisha picked up her diary from the study table and brought it to Pragya, opening it to a page.

'Just read that highlighted portion,' Aarisha said sitting down beside Pragya.

Pragya complied, '*Today, he told me something that made me love him even more, if that's at all possible. He said he was attracted to the substance that makes me, much more than the skin that covers me!*'

Aarisha explained, 'So you see I don't need to impress him with my outward appearance. I know how much he cares for me.'

'I'm so jealous of you,' sighed Pragya. 'My guy never reads any of my signals, so I have to ask him outright. But that's fine because I don't think he's the ONE,' Pragya lamented.

'But I'm sure he is the one for me, which is why I don't want to fall short on anything.'

After a pause, Pragya asked, 'Hang on, are you guys going to do it tonight? Then I would suggest you wear a dress . . . easy to slip off the essentials, you know. It was a real struggle with Rajat last time. I was wearing skinny jeans, and they were difficult to take off. By the time I did, he had lost his erection.'

'I'm not sure whether we'll do anything of the sort,' laughed Aarisha.

'Why not?'

Aarisha murmured something noncommittal, but Pragya wouldn't let up, 'When was the last time you guys did something? Even if not all the way . . . a kiss perhaps?'

'I don't remember. But it did happen.'

'You don't remember, but it happened? That same old shit?'

'Yes, the same shit. I made a note of it in my diary, but I just don't remember it happening,' Aarisha picked up the diary and flipped a few pages to indicate a particular entry.

Dear Diary,

Finally, after waiting for so many months, he was here today. And we kissed. I loved the way he chewed on my lower lip and caressed my tongue with his. Slowly, gently, sensually. The feel of the stubble on his cheeks, his breath soft on my face . . . damn, why didn't time just congeal into a freeze frame then and there?

'I'd rather die than forget such a sensual encounter,' said Pragya before she realized that she shouldn't have said it. 'I'm sorry,' she went on hurriedly, striving desperately for damage control, 'I know you'll get better.'

Aarisha sensed a barrage of negative thoughts within her mind. Not tonight, she thought determinedly and stood up.

'Forget it,' Aarisha went to the large full-length mirror and pirouetted. 'Alright, one final, final time. Is this all right?'

'If I looked even half as good as you do right now, Rajat would call me *maal-pua* (a syrupy Indian pancake dipped in thickened milk).'

'Maal-pua? The sweet?'

'His favourite sweet. But the "maal" part is . . .'

'Okay, okay I got it. Rajat has a weird sense of humour. I don't think Vanav would ever call me "maal".'

'Naturally. You're his Ranisa, after all, the queen of his heart,' Pragya teased.

Aarisha blushed. She heard a car honk outside her house. 'The driver has come.'

'At her majesty's service,' Pragya laughed.

'Come on, I'll drop you off at home before I meet him.'

Vanav had already arrived at their rendezvous. After the car dropped her at the end of the lane, she walked down the verdant path towards the gleaming river.

She saw the flicker of a torchlight just before her cell phone buzzed. 'Follow the flashlight,' said Vanav's message. Aarisha did as asked.

Vanav was sitting on a large boulder by the riverbank, but immediately stood up when he saw her approach, 'I hope you had no problem getting here?'

'Not at all,' she said, trying to secure her hair that was blowing around in the breeze.

'You seem nervous. Don't be,' said Vanav, reaching for her hand.

'You said it's a date, so I decided I needed to look my best,' she shrugged and smiled.

'You look great. And anyway, the best really doesn't matter when someone is in love with your worst.'

'You always make me feel so special,' whispered Aarisha shyly.

'Because you are special,' Vanav caressed her cheek, brushing away her flyaway hair, his thumb grazing the nose stud. She had slipped on the nose stud in the car because she didn't want to show it to Pragya. Somehow it had felt a little too personal to share with her bestie.

'Thanks for wearing this.'

'Why this nose stud in particular?'

'The "why" isn't important. Not anymore. I've planned something special for you.'

He held her hand, his grasp as always tight enough for her to feel assured and loose enough to feel safe. *He is all about that delicate balance.*

Vanav stepped into a small boat moored along the river before helping her into it. They sat facing each other and he started rowing. She realized the water wasn't flowing very much so Vanav's skilful oarsmanship propelled them along quite swiftly through the water.

Aarisha hadn't realized that a date in the heart of nature, with the water gently lapping at the sides of the boat, would be so romantic.

'Where are we going?' she asked. There was nobody in sight for miles around. She felt like they were two lonely souls, intertwined by a cosmic force.

'We are where we have to be. So, we don't go anywhere from here. We stay.'

Cryptic talk, another trait of his, she thought. He was like a painting where things were more concealed than revealed. Every time a dimension was uncovered, she could rest assured that another was yet to be discovered.

The boat was afloat in the faint current of the sluggish river. He brought out a candle from a picnic hamper that lay by his feet and lit it before carefully sticking it with hot wax on the side of the boat. Vanav took out an elegant bottle from the hamper and said, 'Napa Valley wine.'

She nodded, smiling, her face aglow in the flickering candlelight. Vanav uncorked the bottle deftly and poured it into wine glasses. He extended one glass to her. She took it and said, 'It's my dream to swim naked with you in this river.'

Vanav gave her a prolonged look, knowing well how good a swimmer she was, and said, 'One day, some day.'

'May I come over to your side?' she asked.

Vanav helped her get up and move towards him, while the boat rocked slightly. They sat down again, her back against his chest. Their glasses clinked and time seemed to stand still.

'This is amazing,' she sipped the heady wine.

'The "wow" factor will happen in . . .' Vanav looked at his watch, counted down from fifteen and then snapped his fingers. Aarisha's jaw fell open at the sight: a narrow iridescent line of fire appeared on the water in a circle around the boat.

'Space. Earth. Water. Fire. Air. The five elements of nature. The sixth being my love for you, Ranisa.'

She skimmed her fingers over his arm until she touched his hand, the hand of an artist. The hand he used to perform surgeries on the human body. He caressed her face. She suddenly bit down hard on his forearm.

'Fuck, doesn't it hurt?'

'It does,' replied Vanav. 'But I've trained my mind to ignore pain.'

Aarisha immediately kissed his arm, 'I want you to make me a promise tonight.'

'Tell me.'

'I can't bear your absence, so don't leave me alone for so long.'

'This may sound clichéd,' he laughed, 'but haven't you heard, absence makes the heart grow fonder? I'm here, Ranisa, whenever you need me.'

She placed her wine glass by her feet and looked at him. Their lips were almost touching.

'Will you make love to me, Vanav?'

He went completely still, and she wondered whether she had said the wrong thing. It was only when he raised his hand to touch her face again that she noticed he was wearing a glove. Aarisha's world slowly blurred and then she fell unconscious on his lap. He patted her cheek a few times, but she didn't wake up.

'I'm sorry, Ranisa,' he whispered. The date was over. Vanav continued to sit there, holding Aarisha, until the flames around the boat subsided.

4

PANCHSHEEL PARK, NEW DELHI

Hurry up. Don't keep me waiting, Thakur sahab. Come to me soon.
The audio on the laptop played a female voice in a loop, echoing on the connected woofers. And they heard it; they too were ready. Blindfolded. Standing naked in front of each other. As they heard the words, Vanav started feeling her curves. The more his fingers caressed her, the more her skin prickled with gooseflesh. She took a step closer to feel his breath on her face. It made her feel like it had always done since the first time. It felt like someone was calling her home. Then the kisses happened . . .

Kiss me, kiss me all over. She thought but didn't say it aloud. They weren't allowed to talk during this moment. The silence they maintained between them during such a moment was akin to that in any sacred place. He started kissing her gently on her forehead, her nose, her cheeks, her chin and then slowly went down, kissing her on her bosom, her navel, her thighs and then he flipped her suddenly. He started kissing his way up till he reached her lips, pursed them with his and their mouths started conversing in the language of passion.

Hurry up. Don't keep me waiting, Thakur sahab. Come to me soon.

Vanav picked her up and took her to bed. He remained on top of her. His eyes were blindfolded but he could see her. Those greyish-blue eyes, the mole on the chin, the oval face . . . Vanav started rubbing his face against hers. He felt her arms around him and legs around his waist.

Hurry up. Don't keep me waiting, Thakur sahab. Come to me soon.

This experience wasn't an eventuality of lust. For lust only makes you believe it's about a specific person which it never is. It's always about the physical urge. The person becomes the medium. For sex is the basis of what we are. Love is the basis of what we become in life. This experience was about a certain kind of love which is pure, undoubtedly, but can't come out in the open. It's not illicit in its thought but once confessed, by either involved, it can turn it into one. It's a kind of love which brings with itself a bond, not necessarily a relationship. And unlike the latter, bonds don't have rules. It's just there beyond anyone's control. The person with whom you share the bond may not be with you physically, you may not see or hear the person for years and yet you know the person is somewhere within you waiting to be heard, waiting for your deepest fears, your darkest confessions, waiting to know you in your most vulnerable moment. And you share. You share every bit with that person who lives within you but whom you rarely meet or see or hear.

Hurry up. Don't keep me waiting, Thakur sahab. Come to me soon.

Vanav entered her. Her body had turned warm. He knew that happened whenever she cried. He knew why she was crying but he wouldn't probe. This wasn't a bond. This was a relationship. A relationship between two broken humans who had been nursing each other for years now. Thus, it had rules which both respected.

As Vanav began his thrusts the images of his house in Ajmer, the terrace where Aarisha had danced, the Dargah Sharif where he had once wished for her, the *chaat wala*, the train journey, that look on her face when she told him it wasn't possible and that tattoo began to flit through his mind . . .

'Ranisaaaa!' Vanav hollered out.

She held him as tightly as she could. His body shuddered. Only she knew it wasn't because of pleasure. It was because of the pain which he was taking to his grave. The room was silent. And then the female's voice was heard again.

Hurry up. Don't keep me waiting, Thakur sahab. Come to me soon.

Vanav removed his blindfold. He always felt emotionally exhausted after such sessions. And yet he couldn't live without them either. Moving away from her, he switched off the audio.

'Thanks,' he whispered to the girl.

She craved for a hug but didn't say it. She only smiled back. 'Give me some time,' she said stepping out of the bed, naked.

Vanav didn't look at her. Seeing her go inside the washroom, he wore his underwear.

In the washroom, the girl sat on the toilet and broke down completely. There was nobody to blame because she herself had chosen suffering to be her happiness.

5

Dear Diary,

Last night we were on a boat on the Tosh river. He and I, along with the five elements of nature. It's difficult to describe how magical it felt to be so isolated in the world with just one other soul beside me. We sipped wine, kissed and then made love. He stripped me, gently, layer by layer, I was feeling both shy and aroused. As soon as I was naked, I hugged him tight wanting to fuse into him. And then it happened. He started kissing me. I blush to even put it all down in words. I'm so happy that it happened at long last. I had always complained to him about keeping me at arm's length, but he finally fulfilled my innermost desires.

The diary entry made no sense to Aarisha. She couldn't remember anything that had happened but the words in the diary clearly indicated that they had made love. Why didn't she remember it? Was this also because of the 'incident'? Weren't the medicines working?

'Come down, beta, breakfast is ready,' she heard her mother call from downstairs.

'Coming!' She stowed the diary in the drawer in her study table and lightly ran down the stairs.

It was mouth-watering—hot *aloo parathas* with curd for breakfast. Her father read his newspaper while her mother poured out the tea before sitting down beside her. Dude thumped his tail on the floor, looking forward to the tasty titbits that would make their way under the table.

'Won't you ever tell me why I need to take all these medicines?' Aarisha asked.

Her parents exchanged a troubled glance, before her father spoke, 'There was a bad incident.'

'That's what you say every time I ask. What bad incident? I lost my years of college. My friends are all ahead of me. I feel . . . I feel stupid because I don't know about my own life.' Aarisha pushed away her plate and stormed out. She wheeled out her bicycle from the porch and called out, 'I'm off to the café.'

Before her parents could say anything, she was already gone. Dude stood up, shook himself and then lay down again.

'Next time she asks,' said Mr Shergill, 'just tell her it was an accident.'

'We should have told her about it a long time ago,' Mrs Shergill argued.

Mr Shergill merely shrugged and went back to his newspaper.

Tosh as a tourist spot had gained traction recently due to Aarisha's efforts. 'Words and Whims: A Creator's Café' had benefitted greatly from Aarisha's social media skills. The coffee shop included a small library, a corner to sketch, an area for pottery, and a stylish, modern kitchenette island for tea and coffee bang in the centre. Aarisha had taken it over from her parents and expanded and improved it vastly, creating online accounts for the café which she meticulously updated. She invited tourists to both follow and post pictures using hashtags. Ramprasad, her man Friday, was an invaluable assistant. He ensured that the café opened and closed like clockwork. And on a fortnightly basis he even sallied forth to the city to stock up on groceries.

Ramprasad greeted her as Aarisha hurried over to the counter and started checking the sheaf of invoices. A young American couple were exploring the quirky, offbeat features of the cafeteria. The man asked Aarisha whether the pottery facilities were free.

'Of course! It's a creator's café. We'll write your name on whatever you create and display it in that large glass cabinet over there,' Aarisha waved towards a wall where there were already several paintings and behind the glass were beautiful potteries of various sizes, shapes and colours, all of which were labelled with the names of the artists. She ushered the couple to the corner with the potter's wheel and showed them where the raw materials were.

'What can I get for you?' she handed each of them a menu.

After the couple were served their muffins and lattes, Aarisha retreated to the counter and watched them unobtrusively. It was clear that the guy hadn't a clue about pottery, although the girl did seem to know what she was doing. She was trying in vain to teach the guy, but he was, in addition to being all thumbs, a recalcitrant student. They looked incredibly cute together. Aarisha made a mental note of perhaps trying pottery with Vanav one day. The door of the café burst open and three loud youths came in with beer cans, mouthing abuses, laughing raucously and ribbing each other.

'Excuse me,' said Aarisha loudly, 'I'm afraid we don't allow alcohol or outside food here.'

The boys eyed Aarisha and seemed to strip her naked with their glance. It made her feel very uncomfortable.

'Sorry,' said one of the guys. He snatched the cans from the other two guys, looked around for a garbage can and dumped all three beers into it.

'Thanks,' said Aarisha. The boys sat down, their eyes roving over the female clientele in the café.

'Excuse me,' said the same boy who had discarded the beer cans, 'can we have the menu please?'

Aarisha glanced at Ramprasad who sullenly put one on their table.

Aarisha messaged Vanav:

WHEN ARE YOU COMING BACK? I MISS YOU.

Her face fell to see the single tick mark against the message— it had not been delivered. Her existing bad mood only worsened.

'It's not here,' the boy complained loudly.

'I'm sorry?'

'I looked for you on the menu. We wanted to know the rate,' the three louts struck their palms in boisterous high fives and guffawed. The other customers ignored them coldly.

'Perhaps she's priceless.'

'Perhaps free, hence not on the menu.'

Aarisha went over to their table, 'What's your problem?' she asked quietly.

The louts stood up. 'Nothing. We're gone.'

'Good.' As she turned away, Aarisha felt a hand slap her buttocks.

'There was a fly,' he said insolently. Aarisha fumed but held her peace because she didn't want to make a scene in the café. Truth be told, she was a little scared. The three boys, laughing among themselves, left the café. Ramprasad had telephoned her father by then.

Aarisha returned to the counter, her body trembling with rage. Vanav's name flashed on her phone. She answered the call and burst into tears.

The Tosh river's banks glistened in the silvery moonlight. The three youths who had harassed Aarisha were sitting by a boulder, having beer, smoking weed and cracking bawdy jokes when they heard clanking. They turned around to see a man at a distance in the light of the moon. He appeared to be carrying what looked like heavy chains. The man secured the chains around the smaller boulders.

'Piss off, motherfucker! You're interrupting our moonlight picnic,' hollered one of the inebriated louts.

Without a word, Vanav pulled out a revolver from his pocket and screwed on a silencer. At the sight of the gun, the boys dropped their beer in alarm and stood up.

'Whoa, calm down, man. You can totally use this space. We were just leaving.'

'Who touched the girl?' Vanav asked.

For a moment, they were all at sea, 'What?'

'The girl in the café. Who touched her?'

Two gestured towards the third guy who was wringing his hands together, 'I'm sorry, dude. I really am.'

'Men like you are never sorry. You need to be made to feel sorry,' Vanav said and gestured with the gun, indicating that his two cronies move aside. 'Come here.'

Nobody moved.

'Do you want my gun to do the talking?'

The terrified hooligan came over to Vanav.

'Fasten these around your ankles,' Vanav said. It was a pair of handcuffs linked to the chained boulder. The boy obeyed, rapidly descending from his cannabis and beer high. Vanav produced two more pairs of handcuffs and ordered the other boy to tether themselves to each other with the handcuffs around their ankles, a length of gleaming chain between them. The boys were now freely wetting their pants in terror.

'Now jump in the river,' Vanav's voice was icy.

The boys were petrified.

'We don't know how to swim,' confessed one of them.

'I'm not your mother to give a fuck about what you do or don't know.'

When they didn't move, Vanav went over and yanked the louts, chained to each other, to the water's edge. Vanav's incredible strength took him by surprise. The youths held back, cringing and whining.

Vanav turned around and snapped, 'One more squeak out of you and I'll shoot you in the head and dump you in the river.'

He ruthlessly dragged the two weeping lads and pushed them into the river. The boulders tethered to the chain sank without a trace dragging the unfortunate louts into the depths of the river. The silence was deafening.

Vanav turned to the remaining romeo who had passed out.

A few hours later, he woke up, his eyes adjusting to the moonlit nightmare that had not ended. Vanav was sitting beside him, waiting patiently.

'Man, I'm really sorry,' he wheedled. Vanav reached out and grabbed his hair cruelly; the boy screamed. A filthy rag was thrust into his mouth. The struggling youth realized that his arm had been twisted behind him and was cuffed to his ankles. Only his right hand was free. Vanav put a photograph on a boulder in front of him and asked him to take a good look at it. It was the girl in the café, the one he had dared to spank.

'Touch her,' Vanav commanded. The boy shook his head, slobbering. Vanav snarled out the order, a little louder this time. The boy touched the photograph with a trembling forefinger. Vanav sliced off the finger with his military-issue knife. The boy's screams were muffled by the gag.

'Touch her,' Vanav repeated. With tears in his eyes and almost losing consciousness again, he placed another finger of his bleeding hand on the photograph reluctantly. This was ruthlessly hacked off as well. Each of his five fingers were severed. The boy blacked out from the excruciating pain. Vanav removed the gag and tethered the guy's feet to another boulder before dropping him into the river as well. The miscreant sank like a stone.

Vanav cleaned the tell-tale traces of blood off the boulder and collected his belongings before calling the local police station. He told them that he was an army captain who had chanced across an unattended car by the Tosh river.

6

'I don't understand why some people have to be so rude!' Aarisha exclaimed. It was the morning after she had been harassed by the ill-mannered boors in her café. The unpleasant episode preyed on her mind and played over and over in her head on a loop. She had narrated the entire incident to Vanav when he visited the café after Ramprasad's call. He even made an unofficial complaint to the local police station just in case the hooligans returned.

'Some people get a high by bullying others,' Mr Shergill said.

They were sipping tea on the patio. Aarisha had served Dude his breakfast, which he was wolfing down with gusto. Her mother emerged from the inner recesses of the house with the tea trolley on which she had arranged fresh toast, fried eggs, baked beans, tomatoes and mushrooms. 'It's all about the upbringing,' she said, transferring the dishes onto the patio table. 'Nurturing makes such an impact on people that they will always behave with propriety throughout their lives.'

'I agree,' said her husband, buttering a slice of toast.

'I hope those three rot in hell,' Aarisha was still furious, partially with herself for lacking the gumption to retaliate spontaneously.

'Perhaps they already are,' said Vanav.

Aarisha could hardly believe her eyes when she saw Vanav on their doorstep that morning. It was a rare phenomenon when he came to meet her this promptly because there was usually a month's gap between their meetings. 'Why didn't you tell me you were coming?' she asked, flinging herself into his arms.

'I wanted to surprise you,' Vanav grinned.

She held his arm and drew him to the patio at the back of the house. The best thing about their love story, Aarisha thought, was that she didn't have to hide it from her parents. They knew who Vanav was. Surprisingly, she didn't have to introduce him to them either. After the 'incident', as her parents, and later Vanav, had told her, he visited her at the hospital all the time. He had told them who he was. Vanav was the kind of man that no parent would have objected to if he were dating their daughter.

Her father soon excused himself saying he had to get ready to go to the café and her mother also disappeared indoors on some pretext, leaving them alone outside.

'It feels like a dream to see you here today,' Aarisha said.

'We've lived in dreams enough, my love. We are each other's reality now,' Vanav said softly.

Aarisha leaned forward and gave him a quick peck on his cheek.

'I have something for you,' Vanav pulled out a pair of *ghungroo*s from his sling bag and gave them to her. She looked at them with shining eyes.

'Oh my god! These are beautiful.'

'I've arranged for a Kathak dance teacher for you. He'll be here soon.'

'How did you know that I was dying to learn a new dance form?'

'That's what happens when two hearts connect as ours have,' laughed Vanav.

'You're amazing!' she exclaimed.

Dude danced around the table woofing seeing them. 'You're my everything, Aarisha, that's why I am the way I am.' Aarisha's eyes were moist with the joy she felt.

'Sometimes I feel scared. When things are so perfect, it feels good but there is also this, perhaps irrational, fear that perfect things are transient and won't last forever. Do you feel this fear as well?'

'No. I've lived half my life yearning for something I thought I could never have. Now that I have it, I don't have time for fears anymore. I want to live this life without fear . . . Ranisa.'

'Why do you say you've been seeking me half your life?'

'When people are meant to be together, however far apart they are when they're born, their journey towards each other appears before they appear before the other. It's pure magic that makes two apparent strangers meet and realize that they belonged together, forever.'

She looked into his face, mesmerized.

'I'm not your lover,' whispered Vanav, 'I'm your *jogi*. My very life is a spell cast by your love.'

'Sometimes I feel so lucky that I think that if I died right now, I wouldn't complain because my every wish has been fulfilled.'

Vanav hushed her with a finger on her lips, 'Never talk about death in my presence.'

'Is this the Shergill house?' A voice broke into their reverie. It was the dance master.

Aarisha's mother bustled in and conducted them to the terrace where he could train Aarisha. A narrow runner carpet had been laid out on which the instructor sat down and tuned his instruments. Vanav helped Aarisha fasten the ghungroo on her ankles and then left her with the dance master and went downstairs.

Mr Shergill waylaid Vanav at the foot of the stairs. 'I have a request, sir,' said Mr Shergill. Vanav raised an eyebrow. 'My son is ill. I wondered whether I could have an advance on next month's salary.' Mrs Shergill joined him and looked at Vanav pleadingly.

'Sure. I'll transfer both your salaries later today.'

'Thank you so much, sir,' they touched his feet, making him acutely uncomfortable.

'How many times have I told you not to do this?' protested Vanav, drawing away.

'You've changed our lives and we'll always be grateful to you.'

Vanav took his leave abruptly, asking them to tell Aarisha that he would return soon.

Later that day, Pragya came to the café to meet Aarisha. She found her showing some guests the pottery corner. Pragya's animated expression told Aarisha that she was bursting with some exciting news. She excused herself from the guests and turned to her bestie.

'Look at this,' Pragya showed her phone to Aarisha. On the screen was a boy's Facebook profile. His name was Nimish Karwal.

'Who's he?'

'My new boyfriend. He is coming here in a few days.'

'New boyfriend? What happened to—'

'Rajat? Done and dusted.'

'But weren't you in love with him?'

'I thought so. But I think I'm in love with Nimish now.'

'Okaaay!' Aarisha wondered how they could be best friends—she being faithful to the bitter end, while Pragya changed affinities with the same speed that she changed her clothes. Perhaps it was this disparity that made them besties. In the last one year, Pragya had changed four boyfriends and had fallen in love seven times. In the last three instances, that love wasn't even reciprocated. Pragya launched into a description of Nimish, their chats, pictures of his motorbike, the tattoos on his gym-trained body; Aarisha couldn't help but wonder how she and Vanav remained each other's constant. As a contradiction to the volatility of life, the quest for something that was constant and outlived everything, justified one's existence. The epiphany that came with this thought made Aarisha smile. This was a conversation that she needed to have with Pragya one day.

'How do you know that your love for Vanav is real if you haven't tried other guys?' Pragya would often ask.

'The very fact that I don't want to try anyone else tells me that my love for him is real.'

'Don't you think he's a little old for you?'

That was true. There was quite a bit of an age difference. But that couldn't preclude love between them. 'All I know is nobody will or can love me more than he does. For me that answers all my doubts.'

Not that she judged Pragya for guy-hopping all the time. Aarisha knew that Pragya too would stop the moment she sensed it from her core that she had finally got her man. That was the power of true love because it blurs out everything else except for the person.

When Aarisha returned home after shutting shop for the night, she quickly had her dinner and retired to her room. She messaged Vanav:

I MISS YOU.

She opened her diary to pen her thoughts. After her meeting with Pragya in the café, Aarisha felt a sudden surge of nostalgia that made her flip to the page where she had written about her first meeting with Vanav.

That was, as the date suggested, three years ago.

Dear Diary,

I met someone today. An army personnel, Capt. Dr Vanav Singh Thakur. I read the name on his badge. He looked like an Adonis in his uniform. He was alone, seated at a table in our café. I had gone there from college. I couldn't tear my eyes away. There was something weirdly magnetic about his personality. He didn't look at me even once. Most men ogle at me in a ghastly way. I accidentally spilt some of the coffee on his uniform while serving him. Some of the coffee had spilt on my red polka-dotted dress as well. The poise with which he handled the entire embarrassing situation was commendable. When he looked at me before leaving the café, it wasn't a look of discovery. It was a look of recognition. It was as if he had always known me. I felt that familiarity as well. Is that how soulmates feel when they meet for the first time? I hope he visits the café again because I don't know anything about him. But I want to know everything.

Aarisha smiled, revelling in her thought of that day. The memory of that day wasn't very clear and so she read and re-read the diary entry. She suddenly frowned and sat up with a start on her bed. She rushed to her wardrobe. It took her a few seconds to locate the neatly folded dress. It was the one she had been wearing on the day that she had first met Vanav—the one described in her diary entry. But it wasn't a red polka-dotted dress. It was a green polka-dotted dress. She didn't have any other polka-dotted dresses as far as she could remember.

That's odd, she thought. Why would I write a lie about my own dress in my own diary? Or was it just a slip, she wondered.

7

PANCHSHEEL PARK, NEW DELHI

The upper floor of the two-storeyed house was on rent while the ground floor was always kept locked. The owner, an NRI who lived in the US, was hesitant about letting the place out to a single woman, but she assured them that she was married. Her husband, an officer in the army, would drop in on her from time to time when he was granted leave. The young lady seemed earnest enough and the old landlord decided to take a gamble. A year went by without any incident although the landlord was yet to confirm the woman's story about her husband.

It had rained incessantly the previous night and morning dawned with a virginal freshness. The area was generally quiet with only the occasional purr of a car driving past. The girl was in the shower when she heard the squeak of the gate. It had to be Vanav, she guessed. He had messaged her earlier to say that he would be there in the morning. By the time the doorbell rang, she had slipped into a towelling robe, with a fluffy towel wrapped around her head. She opened the door to see Vanav holding two months' worth of groceries in large shopping bags. She quickly took a few bags from him to lighten his load.

'Why do you have to bring everything all at once? When will you start relying on online services?' she chided him.

'You know I'm old school. I already hate the fact that I can't be here as much as I want to, so I don't want to feel additionally guilty about you being in a situation where you don't have something you desperately need.' He walked in and placed the shopping bags on the dining table.

'You're always here, captain,' she teased.

He hugged her immediately. It was easy enough to find a person who was one's strength, but to find a person to whom one could reveal one's vulnerabilities, that was something that happened very rarely.

Samiha had lost her parents and she had intentionally kept a distance from her relatives who were only good at making her feel bad about herself because of her medical condition. Though that was not the only reason she had surrendered herself to Vanav long before he demanded her submission, and not once had she asked for anything in return. It was as if her surrender was what truly defined her. She always knew that they would never have a story of their own; nevertheless, she was reconciled to it. Vanav was aware that a deep-rooted conviction was the only pre-requisite for their love. She made him realize that life would eventually wear people out. But if you could find someone who'd accept you with all your flaws and quirks, then you could be saved. Samiha was that person for him. He knew she was in love with him, even though he wasn't. That was clear between them. They weren't friends either. Nor were they in a relationship of any kind. And yet they were together.

'You're free to choose to be with whoever you like, whenever you like. Just let me know, and I'll back off,' he had said during their first tête-à-tête. Their incredible rapport filled the emotional craters that life creates within people. A connection that didn't need to be defined. All that was needed was a healthy mutual respect for each other's inner wounds and an unconditional affinity for the other.

Vanav had met Samiha during his medical internship. At the time, both were battling deep troughs of depression. As Samiha's father was in the army, she was admitted to the armed forces hospital to be treated for drug abuse and severe agoraphobia that had culminated in attempted suicide. Both Samiha and Vanav were broken beings on some level, so they clicked almost instantly without having to justify themselves to each other.

'I've made my choice, captain, and as you know, I'm a very stubborn girl,' she had told him.

Samiha went into the modular kitchen to sort out the groceries. Vanav went into her living room to examine her latest sketch of him. This was a thing between them. She made pencil sketches and he would fill in the colour whenever he visited. He had asked her why she invariably drew him wearing the exact same expression.

'It's not the same expression,' Samiha protested. 'If you look closely, captain, I'm trying to capture your mien each time you talk about her. Every drawing, therefore, has a minute change from the last. But I'm yet to get there.'

Vanav called out to Samiha from the living room, 'Is this it?'

Samiha nodded, smiling over her shoulder.

'I get the feeling you don't really want to capture that specific expression,' Vanav said.

'Getting there . . . arriving ruins all the fun of trying to get there, don't you agree? Perhaps I'm all about seeking the complete in the incomplete,' Samiha said with a smile.

Vanav noticed that she was making tea for them. He glanced out through the window and noticed that it had started to drizzle. He walked out on to the balcony.

She approached the balcony door and frowned, 'I know why you're out there, captain. Please come back inside.'

'Come here, Samiha,' Vanav coaxed. The last time she had stepped out in the open was two years ago when she had moved into this house, and she alone knew the Herculean effort it had been and the toll it had taken.

'If you don't confront your fears, how will they ever go away? I'm still waiting for my tea,' Vanav smiled and gestured to her invitingly to step out and admire the view from her balcony.

Samiha took a deep breath. Vanav was too stubborn to get off his favourite hobbyhorse once he was astride it. Her hands trembled as she carried out the tea tray, making the teacups rattle. By the time she was on the balcony, she had turned ashen. Raindrops splattered on her neck and arms.

'Captain, can I go back inside please?' Samiha pleaded, her eyes squeezed shut.

'Won't you give me my tea?'

Such was her agoraphobia that with every step it was growing more difficult for her to focus. She felt like she was walking on brittle ice that was beginning to crack under her feet. She wanted to run back screaming into the safety of the house. However, she couldn't disappoint her captain, so she shut her eyes and very, very slowly traversed the distance of four metres until she reached Vanav. The entire exercise had taken her five whole minutes. He gently took the teacups from her and set them aside on the little patio table by the wall. She opened her eyes, leapt on him and wrapped her arms around his neck and her legs around his waist.

'Take me inside, now,' she commanded imperiously, although her voice still trembled.

Vanav, picked up the tray and walked into the living room with Samiha clinging to him. He lowered her into a chair and handed her a cup. He then sat on the floor by her feet and leaned against her knee, sipping his tea.

'The tea must be cold.'

'Don't worry about it,' said Vanav.

Samiha ran her fingers through his thick mane of hair. After a few minutes, she asked, 'How is she?'

'Good,' he avoided her gaze.

'I'd like to meet her sometime.'

'One day . . .' Vanav promised vaguely. 'You know she asks questions for which I have no answers.'

'Questions like?'

'Why I don't make love to her?'

Samiha felt his body shudder and she knew he was crying. 'Captain . . .' she trailed off.

Their unspoken rule decreed that neither of them would stop the other from crying. She hated to see her captain this weak, but she could do nothing to console him. Her role in his life was to allow him to delve deep into his emotional discomforts rather than provide succour.

She rubbed his back and Vanav sat up, raising his head from her lap. She finished her tea and went to her laptop by the bed, unwinding the towel from her wet hair. Her long hair cascaded down her back. She punched some keys on her laptop to play a voice on a loop; and then she turned the volume up.

'*Hurry up. Don't keep me waiting, Thakur sahab. Come to me soon,*' a woman's husky voice reverberated over the speakers.

Samiha then turned around and dropped the bathrobe.

Vanav reached for her, his eyes bloodshot. He touched her forehead with his.

'Won't you make love to me, Thakur sahab?' Samiha asked.

'I will . . . Ranisa . . . I promise you,' Vanav kissed her, their saliva and tears melding together.

8

I always miss you.

It was a message from Vanav in response to hers from last night. She checked the time. She had received it an hour ago. That meant he had been working late again and had gotten to bed only in the wee hours. Although she wanted to call him, she decided against disturbing his sleep, especially because last night she too had had a sleepless night.

Writing 'red' instead of 'green' preyed on her mind and made her toss and turn all night. A diary is the documentation of one's innermost thoughts, a record of things that one can't share with another person, and nobody fibs to one's own diary. So why would she write a different colour unless it was a bizarre error? Aarisha couldn't justify it at all. First thing the next morning, she crossed out the word 'red' in her diary and wrote 'green' over it.

When she went downstairs, her mother told her that her father has gone to Baddi with Ramprasad to buy supplies for the café. Helping her mother with lunch later that day, Aarisha asked her, 'Why don't you guys ever tell me what actually happened to me?'

Mrs Shergill merely shrugged.

'The "incident"—that's what you and papa keep referring to. It was a bad "incident". But what was this bad "incident"?'

'Of course, we have told you,' Mrs Shergill looked shifty-eyed before adopting an ultra casual façade, 'it was an accident.'

'At first, you guys kept referring to it as an "incident", then a "bad incident" and then finally you say it was an "accident". If it was an accident, then how did it happen? That is something you've never told me.'

'Why is it so important? By God's grace you survived. That's all we need to be happy about. Forget the rest of it.'

'I don't remember much. I know my messed-up memory is because of the accident, but today I want you to describe this "accident" to me,' Aarisha sounded annoyed.

Realizing that there was no way that she could distract Aarisha from this topic, her mother said, 'All right. You were on your way home from college and a car hit you. It was a hit-and-run. You were discovered by the police and taken to the hospital before we were informed. You remained in ICU for half a month before regaining consciousness. There, are you happy now?'

Aarisha made a mental note of the fact that her mother had mentioned that she was returning from college. It meant the accident must have happened in Solan for she had been doing her engineering in JUIT, Solan, and was put up in its hostel.

'What car was it?' Aarisha asked.

'The car didn't even stop, so we never found out anything about it. Now, no more questions. Have your lunch, beta, have your medicines and take a nap.'

When Aarisha woke up in the evening, she found that she had a missed call from Pragya and some pictures of her on her phone. All the pictures were of her in the nude. Aarisha called Pragya.

'Please tell me you've not sent those pictures!' Aarisha demanded knowing fully well why her bestie had sent them to her.

'I haven't. I was waiting for you to choose the best one.'

'Firstly, use Photoshop and remove your face from them before sending these out. It's too risky. More importantly, why is it so necessary to share nudes?' Aarisha asked.

'You'll never understand. Not everyone is as boring as your boyfriend.'

'Just because Vanav doesn't ask for nudes doesn't mean he's boring.'

'Yeah, whatever. Now tell me which one.'

'I don't know. Whatever you prefer,' Aarisha said shortly and hung up. Pragya would often get on her nerves like this.

Pragya called again.

Now she'll be sorry, Aarisha thought, and picked up the phone, 'What now?'

'I'm sorry,' said Pragya predictably.

'It's okay. Send the third picture but not before blurring or cutting out the face.'

'No. I'm not sending any nudes. Let him come here first, then we'll see.'

'Mmmm, much better.'

'Come over to my place. I've nicked a beer from my dad's bar at home. We'll share it.'

'Awesome. Give me ten minutes.' Aarisha threw on a dress and was about to head out when her mother called out to her.

'Aarisha, your friend is here.'

She frowned. Pragya had invited her over. So why would she come here. She went down and found herself face-to-face with a girl. It took her a few seconds to remember her name: Sandhya. Sandhya had studied with Aarisha in college.

'Hi, Aarisha, how are you?' the girl smiled.

'Hi, Sandhya,' Aarisha hazarded a guess. When the girl didn't react or look startled, Aarisha was relived. The name she remembered was correct. 'I'm good. Nice to see you.' Aarisha couldn't remember how close they were. She made her sit down in the living room.

Her mother bustled around, clucking like a mother hen until Aarisha protested, 'Mom, please!' Mrs Shergill flashed an awkward smile at the girls before retreating into the kitchen.

Sandhya started talking about old times in college which Aarisha vaguely remembered. Sandhya took out an envelope from her bag and gave it to Aarisha.

Even before she extracted the card from the envelope, Aarisha knew what it was.

'Congratulations, Sandhya,' Aarisha said smiling.

'Thanks. D'you remember we always told everybody that even though we were the only girls in college without boyfriends, we would find our life-partners before everyone else. Not that this is a love marriage. My parents agreed to this alliance because—'

Aarisha interrupted Sandhya, 'Was I single when we were in college?'

'We were the only ones who were single in our entire batch.'

'Right.' Aarisha could feel a knot in her stomach. As Sandhya spoke of those days, her conviction scared Aarisha in a strange way.

Mrs Shergill brought in a plate of onion *pakoda* and coffee for the girls and left the girls alone after exchanging a few pleasantries with Sandhya. Aarisha quickly messaged Pragya:

CAN'T COME NOW. SOME WORK IN CAFÉ. CALL YOU LATER.

Sandhya left half an hour later. The moment she left, Aarisha went to her room and took out her diary from the study table and sat down with it on her bed. She leafed through the pages to the initial entries. According to her entries, she had met Vanav when she was in her third year of college. They were a couple by the time she graduated in B.Tech., computer science. Then why the hell did Sandhya say she was single in college? Aarisha could feel the inexplicable knot in her stomach tighten.

9

There was a possibility that her parents didn't know exactly when she and Vanav had become a couple. As soon as Sandhya left, Aarisha did two things.

First, she re-read a few specific entries from her diary, especially the one in which she had written about introducing Vanav to her parents.

Dear Diary,

Today is an important day in my life. The two worlds that I love to death collided today. I was apprehensive about my parents meeting Vanav. What if they disapproved of my choice? I wasn't doubting my choice, but you know how it is. I don't want to live with a person whom my parents dislike. Not as plan A, at least. In fact, I did express my misgivings to Vanav. Perhaps this wasn't the right time. He told me that when one is doing the right thing, the time too is right. Honestly, it was the conviction in his eyes that I relied on. Actually, I thought I would first let my parents know that I have a boyfriend, lay the groundwork and gauge their reaction before actually making the introductions in person. But the way papa and Vanav got along was a treat to behold. I'm so happy today. I hope life goes on like this always.

The date of the entry told her that it was a good five months after her first date with Vanav. Her parents would never have known whether she had been single or not during the time period that Sandhya had mentioned.

Second, she decided to speak to Pragya. She called her right after checking the diary entry.

'When did I first tell you about Vanav?' she asked without preamble.

Pragya was taken aback by the abruptness.

'Don't tell me you don't remember that as well,' Pragya stalled. She had been told by Aarisha's family about her amnesia after the 'incident'. However, Pragya herself wasn't aware of the exact details of the incident.

'Just answer me,' Aarisha prompted her impatiently.

'It was the night before you were supposed to go and meet him, and the "incident" took place.'

Aarisha knew that Pragya didn't know about the accident. But why would anyone conceal an accident and tell people it was a 'bad' incident, she wondered. And not for the first time.

'So, is it possible that I was in a relationship with Vanav and nobody knew about it?' Aarisha articulated the point that was bothering her.

'At least I didn't, because we weren't as close back then as we are now,' Pragya replied.

Aarisha fell silent. First the colour goof up, then this. Was she under some influence while she was penning her own diary entries? she wondered.

'Helloooo, are you still there?'

'The reason why I couldn't come to your place this evening was that Sandhya had come home for a visit.'

Pragya took some time before she said, 'Sandhya Sapru? She left right after college. What's up with her?'

'She's getting married,' Aarisha said.

'Damn, what's wrong with her?' Pragya sounded flummoxed.

'What's wrong with a girl getting married?'

'Yeah, true. Not that I give a fuck what Sandhya Sapru does or doesn't. Although I'm not really surprised that she came over to invite you, and not me. You guys were pretty thick in college.'

Now that she heard her bestie say it, it was a confirmation that perhaps Sandhya and she had been very close. So, Sandhya wouldn't have lied about the other things either. Although Sandhya's narrative didn't quite fit in with the timelines in her diary. She remembered what Sandhya had said when she had asked, 'Why didn't you stay in touch with me?'

'I was told by your parents that something bad had happened to you and that you needed to rest.'

'Anyway, forget all that,' Aarisha heard Pragya say, 'I need your help. I'll come over to your place tomorrow and let you know what this is about.'

'That's fine but I have another question.'

'What's with you today?'

'Shut up and answer me. Was I preparing for the Common Admission Test (CAT) when the accident happened?'

'Accident?'

'I mean when the bad "incident" that happened to me.'

'Yes, of course. We had discussed where we should get our course materials from and then had ordered them together. I finally sat for the CAT last year while you were convalescing but scored miserably.' The last part was said in a guilt-ridden tone of voice.

'Hold on,' Aarisha said, rummaging through her desk and shelves. There was not a single course material for CAT there.

She asked her parents about it during dinner as soon her father was back.

'You were the one who asked us to sell them off because you weren't able to sit for CAT that year,' said her father. 'You said that a new set comes out each year.'

That made sense, unlike some of the other things, Aarisha thought to herself and carried on with her dinner quietly, oblivious to the concerned glances that her parents exchanged.

That night, she had an acute urge to talk to Vanav, but her message to him kept bouncing and she couldn't contact him. An hour later, it reached him, and he telephoned her.

'Hey, Ranisa,' he said the moment she answered his call.

'What are you doing?' she asked.

'Just got done with work. How is it going at your end?' She could never decipher his feelings over the telephone. His tone was always controlled and constant.

'A friend of mine visited me today. Sandhya. She's getting married.'

'That's nice.'

'It made me think about how my friends from college have moved on in life. I checked my Facebook. Everyone is up to something or the other.'

'And . . .'

'I want to study management. I was anyway preparing for the CAT earlier. I think it will not only help me with the café, but also give me some much-needed exposure to the world beyond.' It was something she had been trying to tell Vanav for quite some time. Her life—home-café-home—was becoming excruciatingly monotonous. And now that she knew her friends were all moving on with their lives, there was no reason for her not to do the same. She had recuperated from the accident as well.

'I'll get you all the material in a few days,' Vanav said. This was another thing that always amazed her. He never asked questions or argued or refused her anything. But on the flip side, there were times when she wanted him to squabble. She felt that it would help her get a handle on their relationship. She wanted him to question her sometimes and tell her that her idea was bullshit, even if it wasn't. But that just wasn't to be with her boyfriend. On some level, she was happy about this as well. Pragya would always tell her what a pain-in-the-ass her ex-boyfriend, Rajat, had become, thrusting his choices on her all the time and never allowing her to do anything without subjecting her to a grand inquisition. Pragya once joked after her breakup that leaving Rajat felt like she had walked out of, not a relationship, but an interrogation room.

Aarisha and Vanav talked for a few more minutes and they were about to end the call when Aarisha asked impulsively, 'Can I ask you something weird?'

'Anything.'

'Don't you ever feel like asking me for my nude selfies? Or am I not that attractive enough for that?'

'We used to—' Vanav began.

But Aarisha spontaneously cut the call as a spark of excitement zinged through her. In the next two minutes, she clicked a couple of nude selfies and sent them to him.

Vanav deleted them without even looking at them once. He replied:

NICE!

The monosyllabic, lacklustre response made Aarisha wonder if he didn't like them.

SORRY. WAS THAT DREADFULLY REPREHENSIBLE OF ME? WHEN PRAGYA TOLD ME THAT SHE DID IT WITH HER BOYFRIEND, I MERELY WANTED TO EXPERIENCE IT MYSELF. WAS IT VERY WRONG?

NO, YOU DID NOTHING WRONG. IT'S NORMAL. DON'T WORRY. SOME WORK HAS COME UP AT MY END. LET ME CALL YOU TOMORROW?

DONE. GOOD NIGHT, MY LOVE.

GOOD NIGHT, RANISA.

Vanav wasn't busy working. He had set up camp with a tent and campfire by the river close to the Shergill house. This was where he spent his nights whenever he was in Tosh. He lay on his sleeping bag, sipping from a bottle of wine and listening to a voice on loop on his phone.

Hurry up. Don't keep me waiting, Thakur sahab. Come to me soon.

He flicked his cigarette ash on the freshly excoriated wound on his arm. He wasn't smoking the cigarette; he used it to sustain the masochism which increased his appreciation of the soulful voice. Pain wasn't a by-product of his love for her. Pain was the reason why love happened. And remained forever young.

10

As promised, Vanav got her all the course material for the CAT. He told her that his visits to Tosh would become less frequent because he had been posted to Siachen for a few months. He also told her that, as promised, he had quit smoking. She was delighted to hear about his smoking abstinence, but his news about the new posting made her sulk.

'Why can't you do a normal job?' she moaned. She had invited him for dinner on the last night before he was to travel to Siachen. She had made all his favourite dishes. She had initially contemplated asking him directly about his culinary likes and dislikes, but then realized that her diary entries already had these listed. Reading through her diary, she felt tempted to ask Vanav about the red-instead-of-green polka-dotted dress goof up; but then it was her diary, how would he know about her diary entries? It was unfair to expect him to remember what she was wearing during their first encounter. In all the time that he knew her, he had never once asked to see her diary. He probably wasn't even aware of its existence.

'I know it puts pressure on our relationship but what needs to be done has to be done,' he said gently.

'Just wait until I complete my MBA. I'll open our café in Delhi and then you won't have to work in the army,' she promised.

Vanav chuckled, caressing her cheek and admiring her innocence. Her parents laughed as well. They were glad that Aarisha was back on track with her academics.

'Why not?' Aarisha asked. 'Can't the woman be the bread-winner and her husband, the home-maker?'

'I would happily become a home-maker for you, Ranisa, had I not been serving my country.'

Aarisha pulled a face at that. But she already understood his dedication and loved him for it. After dinner, she drew him out to the terrace for some alone time.

'Thank you for these,' she said, indicating the ghungroo box in the shoe rack by the wall.

Looking at the ghungroo, Vanav wondered whether he should thank her. The sight of her dancing with the ghungroo had changed his life once. She looked into his eyes and then averted them. He sensed something was troubling her.

'What is it, Ranisa?'

'I want us to be a normal couple. All this waiting breaks me somehow. I find it almost unbearable. And then I see Pragya changing boyfriends every six months. And she's so much happier than I am even though I'm the one in a genuine relationship. It makes me question things that I don't want to.'

'We are a normal couple. Just that our "normal" is different,' replied Vanav, cupping her face and caressing her cheeks with his thumbs.

'I just have one simple wish: I want to be with you all the time. Is that too much to ask? I don't know how to live when you aren't around,' Aarisha choked on a lump in her throat. She put her arms around his neck.

Absence . . . I know a thing or two about absence, Vanav thought, but said aloud, 'But do you know the beauty of waiting for someone?'

Aarisha nodded.

'Waiting begets longing. Longing begets certain meaning to your life. And suddenly you realize how useless your life was without understanding the meaning of longing.'

Aarisha hugged Vanav tight and said, 'What if I tell you I want to get married to you soon? Then you'll have to take me to Siachen as well, right?'

His eyes twitched and words ricocheted through his mind: '. . . *We can't be together, Thakur sahab; we can only see each other; we can only feel our absence; but we can't get each other the way we yearn.*' Vanav clenched his jaws to hold back his tears.

'Yeah,' he whispered.

In the months that followed, Aarisha focused on her studies but on weekends there was something else awaiting her.

Pragya and Nimish were going steady. It was a little difficult for Nimish to come to Tosh from Delhi all the time, so they decided to meet at a place which was convenient for both: Dharamshala. He asked her to visit Dharamshala every Friday evening and return to Tosh on Saturday night.

'You have to do this for me,' insisted Pragya. 'And I don't want to hear a no. We'll take the bus. It's just a seven-hour journey. Nimish and his friend from Delhi will be there. It'll be fun.'

'What do we tell our parents? You know they won't allow us to spend the night out.'

'I know. That's why you'll tell your parents that you're sleeping over at my place and I'll tell my parents that I'm sleeping over at yours. They don't call or meet with each other anyway.'

Aarisha's instinct was to say no. But the thrill of going to Dharamshala on her own, away from the monotony, was tempting.

'Come on!' Pragya urged.

'Oh, all right then,' Aarisha said after a beat. She wanted to inform Vanav, but there was no way to contact him immediately, given that they had agreed on a weekly time-schedule for telephone calls. She also feared that his reaction would be the same as her parents if she were to inform them.

Aarisha vowed to abstain from Pragya's company for the rest of the week. However, come Friday, Aarisha couldn't negate the forbidden excitement of the clandestine adventure. Both girls lied to their respective parents as planned and met at the bus stop just in time to take the bus to Dharamshala.

They arrived at their destination on the same night. Nimish and his friend, Deep, who had travelled from Delhi the previous day, reached Dharamshala before the girls.

After checking-in into a hotel, Pragya chose to closet herself with Nimish in the hotel room, making out, while Deep entertained Aarisha, cracking her up with his wonderful sense of humour. He escorted her to the various nooks and corners of Dharamshala, to the little-known eateries and then, when Nimish and Pragya were done, they all met up and drank wine and beer all through the night in the hotel itself. The next afternoon, the girls took the bus to Tosh. On their return journey, Pragya confided to Aarisha about all the lurid details of her bedroom antics with Nimish. On one hand, listening to Pragya made Aarisha long for Vanav; on the other, this newfound freedom was too precious to compromise. Therefore, whenever Vanav called, once in ten or twelve days, she held back even though she desperately wanted to tell him all about her illicit high jinks. She was sure he wouldn't like it, but she couldn't stop herself from joining the fun at Dharamshala either.

Five months later, during one of those weekends, it started raining the moment the girls reached Dharamshala. Nimish and Deep were already in Mountain and Moon, the budget hotel that they always went to. Drenched, the girls managed to reach the hotel. Until dinner the foursome sat cooped up in one room, sharing beers and chatting. None of them realized that they had consumed a lot more alcohol than they usually did.

Before Aarisha and Deep knew what was happening, Nimish and Pragya started kissing and canoodling while Aarisha and Deep were still in the room. When Deep ridiculed their raunchy behaviour, Nimish told Deep to go to his room. The boys always reserved another room for the girls.

Feeling very awkward, Aarisha rose and went into the adjacent room followed by Deep. Aarisha realized her head was spinning with the excess alcohol in her system. She felt like she was losing her self-control. It was only with great determination that she could keep her eyes open. Deep shut the door before tottering to the bed and sprawling on it. Aarisha saw a sofa on the other side of the bed. The remnants of her common sense told her that it was advisable to maintain some distance from Deep since they were inebriated. She sidled past the bed, towards the sofa. However, Deep deliberately tripped her with his leg. When she stumbled, he reached out and yanked her towards him. Aarisha collapsed in a heap on top of him, their limbs in a tangle.

She struggled to get out of his embrace, but he was already planting febrile kisses over her face. Aarisha was aware that something was drastically wrong, but the alcohol in her system weakened her resistance to fight the flow of events. The more she squirmed and twisted, the more she inflamed Deep's desire. His hands roved over her breasts and derrière and, in no time at all, she found herself responding to his kisses with parted lips. He started going down on her, gripping her hands in his, raising her tee with his mouth, kissing her navel. Aarisha mumbled Vanav's name over and over like a chant. As Deep tried to force apart her legs, she summoned all her willpower and kicked him hard. Deep rolled away, exhausted, and didn't approach her again. She wanted to get up and get out of the bed but was too light-headed to do so.

The next morning, when Aarisha awoke, she found herself still on the bed, her clothes partially undone. She quickly made herself respectable. Deep was on the floor by a table. She conjectured that perhaps she had kicked him so hard that he had hit his head on the side-table and had passed out on the floor. The memory of last night made her feel like throwing up. With her heart pounding and moist eyes, she went to the adjacent room. The moment a sleepy Nimish opened the door, Aarisha barged in. She told a half-asleep Pragya that she was leaving for Tosh, grabbed her overnight bag and flounced out of the room. Before her friend could understand what was up with her, Aarisha was already downstairs. She took the first bus in the morning. Pragya messaged her:

WHAT HAPPENED? WHY DID YOU LEAVE SO ABRUPTLY?

Aarisha messaged back:

I'M ALREADY ON MY WAY TO TOSH. COME HOME SOON.

She then scrolled to Vanav's name on her contact list. She wanted to call him, but her hands trembled. She kept repeating to herself 'it didn't happen' even while her tears poured unchecked. If she called him, what would she tell him? That she had unintentionally cheated on him?

When Aarisha was almost home, she saw Vanav standing by the gate, smiling at her. He was holding a huge bunch of roses. He never told her he was coming over. As usual, his presence was supposed to be a surprise for her. Seeing her standing still, he came up to her and hugged her tight, whispering in her ears, 'I'm sorry. I know it has been really long this time.'

A moment later, he broke the hug, realizing the she wasn't responding to his embrace as she usually did. He leaned away to look at her enquiringly.

'I don't deserve you,' she said and broke down, sobbing in his arms.

11

Her parents looked very worried as Vanav ushered in a weeping Aarisha into the house and took her up to her room. He shut the door and gently made her sit on the bed, holding her hand all the while. He placed the bouquet on her study table.

'Tell me what happened? I was told you went to Pragya's place for a sleep-over.'

Aarisha glanced at him and sobbed. He caressed her face, wiping her tears but remained silent.

When her sobs eventually subsided, Aarisha hiccupped and said, 'I was with Pragya, but I wasn't at her place.'

'Where were you then?'

'Every Friday, for the past several months,' her breathing was laboured because of the weeping, 'I told mummy-papa that we were studying at her place, but I didn't go to Pragya's place.'

'Then?'

'We went to Dharamshala.'

'We?'

'Pragya and I.'

'Why Dharamshala?'

Aarisha confessed everything to Vanav, breathing raggedly. When she reached the point in her narration about the previous night, Vanav's jaws clenched hard especially as she told him how they'd got drunk and the way Deep had forced himself on her.

The silence was broken only by Aarisha's rasping breath because her hysterical weeping had congested her nasal passages. She suddenly dropped to her knees in front of Vanav and pleaded, 'Please don't break up with me. I'm truly sorry, I truly am.'

The action took Vanav by surprise and he immediately held her shoulders and raised her to her feet.

'Never kneel down. Not in front of me. Nor anyone. You are a queen. You are my Ranisa. And queens don't kneel,' he kissed her forehead.

'I know this will change things between us. I know it,' she gasped. 'And it's all my fault. I shouldn't have gone with Pragya. Or into that room with Deep. I was so tipsy that I didn't have the least idea of the probable consequences of my stupid gullibility. And now I've gone and fucked my world.'

Still holding her in his arms, Vanav extracted one long-stemmed rose from the bouquet. 'Close your eyes,' he said. She obeyed. He held the rose before her and said, 'Hold this tight now.'

Aarisha closed her fingers around the stem and an involuntary 'ouch' escaped her. Vanav gently unclenched her fingers, dropped the rose and sucked the drop of blood from her finger. She opened her eyes.

'Did it hurt?' he asked. She nodded. 'Did you smell the fragrance of the rose?' Aarisha nodded.

'Love is the simultaneous infliction of pain and the invasion of the divine fragrance. And it is entirely your choice which aspect you focus upon: the thorn or the blossom.'

'Aren't you hurt that I let someone touch me inappropriately?' she averted her eyes as she enunciated the last few words.

'I am. But something else hurt me more. That fact that you lied to me about the night study at Pragya's house. Technically, it's not a lie because you didn't tell me anything; I learnt of it from your parents. I understand why you did what you did. Perhaps you assumed that if you had told me, I would have forbidden it. But when have I ever said no to you? I would have been concerned about the travelling alone part, but I guess I would have agreed to it if it gave you happiness.'

'Please don't say anything more. I can't bear it,' Aarisha choked, feeling guiltier than ever.

'And as someone who has seen a little more of life than you have, just take this as a lesson: more often than not, men will seek you for what they want, and not appreciate what you really have within you. There are exceptions, but then life runs through generalizations, not exceptions.'

'I was sure I had lost you.'

Vanav cupped her face and said, 'It's not so easy to break us,' he kissed her forehead again. She finally felt calm.

It took two whole days for Vanav to track down Deep. Aarisha had mentioned his name. Vanav saw his picture on

Facebook, navigating from Aarisha's profile to Pragya's to Nimish's and finally to Deep's.

Nimish had come down to Tosh after hearing Aarisha's story as relayed to him by Pragya. He apologized to her on Deep's behalf. But Deep had told him that Aarisha had been equally eager to have sex. It was a blurred line and the only witnesses were the ones involved. When Nimish left Tosh, he was oblivious to the fact that he was being followed. He reached Kashmiri Gate in Delhi and then took the metro to his place. He was shadowed right up to the gate of his house.

The next evening, Nimish emerged from his house to walk his dog. Later that night, around nine, he drove to a nightclub in his car. Vanav stationed his car close to Nimish's in the parking lot. At around 1.30 a.m., when Nimish and Deep emerged, the latter began to be tailed. His car was haphazardly overtaken by Vanav in one of the lonely stretches in Noida before screeching to a halt. Deep hurled a barrage of abuses. But the car in front of him had stalled and didn't budge. Frustrated, Deep alighted from his car, walked to Vanav's car and thumped the window by the driver's seat, all set to punch the driver. The window swished down. Deep realized that the driver was wearing a mask. Before he could react, pepper was sprayed into his eyes. Deep broke into a stream of profanities that turned the air blue. He felt a blow on his head and fainted. He was dragged into his own car. Within the next hour, Vanav skilfully amputated Deep's lips using a surgeon's scalpel and left him bleeding in his car.

'If you don't respect women, you shouldn't be allowed to know what it feels like to kiss them,' he whispered in his ears before he got out of Deep's car and drove off in his own. The fact that he had taken Deep's wallet and other valuables made it look like a mugging gone horribly wrong.

When Pragya told Aarisha about Deep's situation, she felt that it was karma doing its job. Pragya never asked Aarisha to accompany her to Dharamshala again. Aarisha realized how much she must have hurt Vanav. She vowed never to hide anything from him ever again and renounced alcohol, unless she was drinking with Vanav.

A month later, Aarisha cracked the CAT and secured a seat in a management institute. It was in a city from which Vanav always wanted to keep her away: Udaipur.

12

PANCHSHEEL PARK, NEW DELHI

'I didn't tell you something,' Vanav said.

Samiha's fingertips stopped making the pattern against the mist laden windowpane. They were sitting on a couch by the window, facing each other. Her fingers on the windowpane stopped for a trice, then continued. She couldn't ask him what it was that he didn't tell her. She could only wait for him to come out with it. Whenever they made love, they became each other's emotional vent but when they told each other things which the other didn't have any direct involvement in, they turned into soul-confidantes bereft of reaction or opinions.

'She is re-locating to Udaipur. She cracked her management exams,' Vanav said.

Samiha turned to face him completely.

'She wants to study further. She wants to explore. She wants to move away from the monotony of Tosh.'

'Rightly so,' Samiha murmured.

'Yes, rightly so. It's not that I hadn't thought about it. But I kept hoping that it would be delayed. Just the way it was necessary to force the bad incident in her life so she remained dependent on me. Emotionally and otherwise. Just the way I kept hoping all my life that she was mine.'

'May I say something?' Samiha asked. Vanav nodded.

'Maybe she is yours. How we belong to people, and people belong to us, can't always be defined. I think Ranisa and you always belonged to each other, but there's a difference between belonging and becoming someone's. People often think becoming is the same as belonging. A stupid mistake we make.'

Vanav drew his legs away from her body, stood up and went to the centretable, picked up the cigarette packet and the lighter and came back to the couch. As he put a cigarette in his mouth, he heard Samiha say, 'I'm sorry but didn't you promise her you won't smoke.'

Vanav glanced at her, lit the cigarette and gave it to Samiha. She took a puff.

'Togetherness is as transitory as this cigarette. Sooner or later it ends. And all of us doggedly seek a permanence in the transitory experience. This location shift will expose her to things which she should organically do at her age and not what I subject her to. I know I've been selfish but—'

'You haven't been selfish, captain,' Samiha cut him off. 'And even if you have, then you have done it after you earned that selfishness. No man ever lets the woman he loves to just be. You have let her be without compromising your love for her. The way you love someone can be of two types is what I've come to understand. One is how you allow a sapling to grow into a plant. You don't stop or intervene in its growth; you water it, allow it sunshine, feed it, and love it however it grows, accepting in your heart the wishes which the sapling couldn't suffice while becoming a plant. The second type is to force the sapling to become a certain type of plant which isn't its core. It's so called growth becomes its death in that case. It's ingrained in men's subconscious that they need to take charge of us. Not let us be what we are but force us to fit into who they think we are. We don't need that. Nobody does.'

Vanav listened to her quietly. Seconds after she was done, he said, 'Someone recently forced himself on her.'

'What?'

'I've taken care of the person but that's not the end of the problem. She will go out, meet new people. Some will come close to her and she may also feel inclined to grow close to a few of them.'

'Insecure?'

'No!' Vanav gave her a sharp look. 'I've spent half my life craving for her touch and to hear her voice. I can't allow myself such privileges like insecurity. It's just that I'll never have answers to certain questions about her.'

Samiha understood what he was talking about.

'Even if I answer them . . . I'm sure she'll slip away from me one day. And once again I'll be back to where it all started. And I must live a life being a nobody to her even though I can give my life for her. It's okay if I mean nothing to her but I don't know what I'll do that day. Or thereafter, except for ending . . .'

Samiha leaped towards him dropping the cigarette and put her finger on his lips.

'Don't say it ever, captain. There's always someone else's life associated with yours. Whether you acknowledge it or not.'

'I'm sorry, Samiha.'

'As I always tell you—you are the perfect partner, captain,' Samiha said. *Whom I will never have*, she finished the sentence in her mind.

'Only till she learns the truth . . .' Vanav said, their gaze fixed on each other. 'Do you think she will understand how much I love her after she knows the truth?'

Vanav tried to smile but tears fell from his eyes.

Samiha took her time before answering. 'I don't think she should ever know the truth, captain.'

13

Aarisha had to make two trips to the MBA institute in Udaipur. Once for the group discussion and interview and the second time, for her admission procedure. Both times, Vanav accompanied her.

He had been transferred to Lucknow's command hospital by the time Aarisha cracked the CAT.

What intrigued her more than the MBA admission procedure was that even though they put up at the same hotel, Vanav booked them into two separate rooms. Although Aarisha cudgelled her brains, she couldn't come up with a satisfactory explanation. Vanav was her boyfriend after all. Even if he shared a room, or a bed, with her, she wouldn't have complained. They had made love so many times. If it happened one more time, how did it matter? On the contrary, she would have loved it. It would have given her that domestic feel: living with the one you love, registering his quirks and eccentricities, noticing little things about him which perhaps even he wasn't aware of and thereby knowing him spool by spool. Lying on her hotel room bed she wondered whether the incident in Dharamshala still rankled him. She didn't voice her doubts to him, however.

Then, she asked herself the ultimate question: if she had discovered that Vanav had cheated on her, what would she have done? Her first instinct would be to scratch, claw and mutilate the other woman. Then, perhaps, she would kill Vanav. But what did he do? Told her that he would respect her happiness above all even if being unfaithful to him was what made her happy. The very thought made her feel about two inches tall. Here was a person who was making her live out the best love story there could ever be and what did she do? She swore to herself that she wouldn't ever put herself in any situation that compromised her feelings for him. And if he was maintaining a distance because of the hurt, he had the right to. Or so she concluded. She would give him time and space, Aarisha decided, but that didn't mean she won't much about it herself. How could she heal him if he was already deeply hurt, but wasn't telling her about it? It was a conundrum for which she couldn't find an answer.

Aarisha shifted into the girls' hostel on a room-sharing basis as soon as the admission procedure was over. Her roommate was Soni. She was from Indore and had a peculiar penchant for homeopathy pills for any and every real or imaginary ailment. She believed everything that happened in her life, however inconsequential, was because it wanted to make her sick. So, she had medicines for everything.

'You're so lucky,' said Soni at their first meeting, 'your brother is so caring. My brother didn't even come to drop me off. I travelled all by myself from Indore. Couldn't even go to the loo. It was so pathetic. I would have caught some urinary tract infection for sure.'

It took a few seconds for Aarisha to realize that Soni was referring to Vanav.

'Excuse me! He isn't my brother. He's my boyfriend.'

Soni gave her an incredulous look. 'Damn, he must love you very much. I haven't seen a boyfriend do so much. If I'm not wrong, he was there during your group discussion as well, wasn't he?'

'He was.'

'If not the brother bit, at least I got the "lucky" part right,' she laughed and swallowed a few pills from a small bottle.

'What are those for?'

'To avoid indigestion from the canteen food here.'

They were yet to check out the canteen. Aarisha was baffled about the girl's intake of medication in anticipation of an ailment. She decided she had to prepare herself mentally because she had to live with this strange girl for the next two years.

Being in a new city, meeting new people and getting into a new schedule made her look forward to life in a different way. Suddenly, Aarisha's life was filled with sleepless nights because of assignments, late night beer parties in dorms, attending lectures and making presentations. She became part of the college's literary society. Although there were a few male batch mates and seniors who showed an interest in her, after what happened in Dharamshala, she was extra careful with boys. She had a phrase ready to keep them at arm's length: 'I'm deeply committed to someone.'

Every time she said that to a guy, she felt virtuous and happy. It was only now, busy as she was with her studies, that she understood why Vanav, who always told her he had work, wasn't available on the telephone most of the time. They usually connected during the night on the telephone for a half-hour chat after she was done with her assignments and when Vanav was also free. She contacted her parents almost daily, updating them with her everyday happenings.

One night, when she emerged from her shower before retiring to bed, she came into the room and found Soni reading her diary. She snatched it from her hand, 'Where are your manners, girl? You're not supposed to read someone's personal diary,' Aarisha snapped.

'I know. I'm sorry, but I couldn't stop myself. It was open and it was about . . .' Soni trailed off, looking embarrassed. Aarisha had forgotten to close her diary before going into the shower. One of her favourite pastimes was to re-read the diary entries where she'd written about Vanav and their lovemaking before stepping into the shower and imagining it in all its pleasurable details. Fortunately, or unfortunately, she couldn't rely on her memory for these minutiae. Her imagination was her only way to relive those intimate moments.

'Your boyfriend is damn creative,' Soni said.

Aarisha sensed the glumness in her voice. Soni had a long-distance boyfriend, a corporate lawyer who lived in Chennai. She hadn't seen him even once during the three months of their time here in the hostel.

'As if you guys have never done it,' Aarisha retorted, still holding on to the diary.

'We have. But it's not half as exciting as yours. Moreover, he never brushes before smooches. It always makes me wonder how much bacteria I am consuming in one kiss.'

Aarisha wanted to laugh but checked herself as she listened to Soni continue, 'Ummm, what do I do to get him to change positions and try different stuff? He is so stuck doing just the one.'

'I've no idea! I've never urged Vanav for such things. It just happened naturally,' Aarisha replied, but in her heart, she realized that she didn't remember any of those 'exciting' experiences either, although she had written it all down. She put the diary in her wardrobe and locked it securely.

She heard Soni say, 'But sex isn't everything, right?'

If Pragya had been here, Aarisha thought to herself, she would have surely commented that that depended on how much sex one was getting. But Aarisha merely nodded in agreement.

'Although he hasn't come to meet me here, and I do miss the sex part a bit, he did take me to meet his parents once. They were really nice. When a boy introduces a girl to his parents, it's a sure sign that he is serious about the relationship.'

Aarisha had switched off the lights in her section of the room. As she lay there, darkness shrouding half her body, she wondered why Vanav hadn't introduced her to his parents. She couldn't remember clearly whether he had told her about them or if she had even met them. As soon as Soni fell asleep that night, Aarisha took out her diary and opened it to the only entry where his parents were mentioned.

Dear Diary

It's always fascinating to know about your partner's roots. Vanav told me today that he was born and brought up in Ajmer. He has his roots in Rajasthan. Perhaps that's why he calls me 'Ranisa'. It's the way the Rajasthani people address their queen. I told him I would love to meet his parents. He promised me that it would happen soon. I looked for pictures of girls in traditional Rajasthani wear and they look so elegant. I imagined myself in the Rajasthani attire. I think I can carry it off really well. I was wondering what it would be like to be with him in the desert. Only him and me and miles of nothingness around. Damn, I look forward to it already.

This diary entry had been made a year and a half ago. If she had met his parents after this, she would have definitely recorded it in her diary, Aarisha concluded.

When he called her the following weekend, the first thing she asked was, 'Where is your family? I want to meet them.'

'Why? What happened?' Vanav asked.

'Nothing. Can't I just meet your family?'

There was a pause before he said, 'My parents are no more.'

'Oh, I'm sorry to hear that. Have you told me this before, or do I not remember it?'

'Yes, I've told you this before.'

'I'm so sorry, Vanav. I thought I must have asked you about them because there's a mention of them in my diary.'

'It's all right. Are you taking your medications on time?'

'Yes, I am.' After a pause, she added, 'I was wondering how it would have been if that accident hadn't happened to me?'

'What accident?' Vanav asked.

'The accident because of which I have amnesia.'

'Oh yes, that accident.'

'I would remember so much more about us, wouldn't I?'

Vanav could sense the remorse in her voice.

'Memories become important only when the person isn't physically present around you. We don't need to care for memories because we are already with each other.'

'Don't you feel frustrated with me? For example, I don't even remember things about us. You know, sometimes I feel you love me more than I could ever love you. Not that I don't want to. I do. But I feel that no matter how hard I try; I will always fall short.'

'There's nothing called "little" love or "a lot" of love, Ranisa. Love is love. The limitations which arise are the limitations of the person, not of the love. Not everyone can live up to this gigantic and mysterious concept.'

'When did you fall so deeply in love with me?' Aarisha asked.

'I've gone beyond the why, when and how. I know I love you. And I want to just keep doing that. Loving you. You are my everyday choice.'

'I want to bring my love for you to this level one day—where nothing matters but the fact whether I'm loving you enough or not. With you I've understood that the basic question couples should ask themselves every day is: Am

I loving the other enough? It's so easy to find fault in the other but to keep pushing oneself to be a better version so that the relationship also becomes better, or should I say more refined, one day at a time, is what one should seek as a personal relationship goal.'

'I'm glad you realized it. But as I told you earlier, I'm not your lover, Ranisa, I'm your jogi, your devotee. You have to be a devotee to be able to do that. And that path isn't easy. And there's a reason why it isn't easy.'

'Why?' Aarisha asked, curious.

'To become someone's devotee, one has to totally deconstruct one's self. Mainly, the ego. Fight all one's natural instincts and the interpretations that one has had to date. Often, it's one's own self that comes in between the togetherness one builds for years. And then everything implodes. The day you consciously make the "I" take a back seat; you stop being just a lover. You become a . . .'

'Devotee, *jogan*,' Aarisha completed softly.

'Yeah.'

'Thank you so much for everything. I don't know what I would do without you.'

And I couldn't have lived without you, Vanav thought, but said, 'Love is always in the actions, Ranisa, not in the words. If I were to say "I love you", then I had better demonstrate it in my actions.'

'Even if you won't say it I know I hurt you with that Dharamshala incident. I couldn't prove my love for you by pulling out of it. I allowed him access to something that is yours: my body.'

'I think people always get it wrong, Ranisa. When we love someone and we share our body with someone else, we think that the purity of our love has been defiled. Why? I think our body is ours. It can't belong to anybody else ever, no matter how many times we share it with someone else. Even if it involves sharing it with the one we love. You can talk about the morality involved, but you can't question the purity of the body. It's only the soul that can belong to someone else other than the self. And honestly, my dear, we don't decide who will start owning our soul. It just happens, and when it does, we simply accept it, willingly.'

'I promise that I'll never do anything that could hurt you in any way ever again. I know my actions were questionable.'

'I trust you, Ranisa. And when I say "trust" it doesn't mean I won't question your actions ever. It's the intention that matters. If you'd intentionally slept with that guy it would have been a different scenario. If you had intentionally slept with him and then lied to me that it hadn't been intentional, it would have been a different scenario compared to your being drunk and taken advantage of. But I do want to tell you something . . .'

'Tell me.'

'Hurt me as much as you want to or can, I won't complain one bit. But never insult my love for you. I won't be able to take it because my love for you is my faith. And nobody should insult another's faith.'

There was a long silence.

'Sometimes I feel I don't deserve all this,' Aarisha said softly.

'We don't decide what we deserve from others. We can only choose what we deserve for ourselves.'

Twenty days later, Soni and a few other girls planned to visit the Dargah Sharif in Ajmer. The moment Aarisha heard the name, she not only told them that she was in, but also messaged Vanav to say that she was going to Ajmer the following weekend. She asked for his address so that she could see the house where he grew up.

Vanav read the message an hour later. He thought for a while. Nature versus nurture. He had read in a medical journal that nature always won in the end. His plan was slowly coming apart at the seams. Not so much that it would become irreparable; but he had to be very careful. His entire stratagem was driven on misinformation. Vanav messaged her his address knowing fully well that he couldn't let her visit the place on her own. Because his parents were very much alive.

14

As soon as Aarisha and her friends were done visiting the Dargah Sharif, the girls wanted to do some sightseeing. Aarisha wanted to visit Vanav's home. She told them to meet her in the central market point in an hour and, using the GPS on her phone, she made her way to the address that Vanav had provided. She used the hired car in which they had driven from Udaipur to Ajmer, while the girls decided to traipse across to the nearby market.

Aarisha was almost at the house when she began wondering what she would do when she eventually got there. His parents were dead, and she didn't even know whether someone lived there or not. She decided she would click a selfie in front of the house and then would probably join her friends in the market square.

When the car stopped in front of the house, Aarisha alighted and checked the address in the message she had received from Vanav with the one etched on the marble slab on the gate post in front of the house. They matched perfectly. The slab read: Pratap Singh Thakur. That was Vanav's father. She wasn't sure whether she should open the gate or not, so she turned on her mobile phone's camera and was just framing herself with the house as a backdrop for a selfie, when, before she could click, a man photobombed her shot, standing on the other side of the gate.

'What the hell!' exclaimed an astounded Aarisha.

'Ranisa visiting my home and nobody to welcome her! How is that even possible?' Vanav said.

She flung open the gate hastily and hugged him, 'Fuck! Have you done a course in surprising people?'

'Not people. Only you,' he replied smoothly.

Vanav took her inside after instructing the car's driver to park by the gate.

Vanav showed her every nook and corner of the house, especially his room. She saw his parents' picture, his family photographs and his childhood pictures. In one of the pictures, she saw a girl with him.

'Who is she?'

'That's Binny. She used to be my best friend.'

'Used to? What happened?'

'We lost touch,' Vanav lied.

'I wish we were best friends as kids. I wish we knew each other from the time you lived here as a kid,' she said wandering on to the terrace.

You did know me then, Ranisa, you did know me, Vanav thought, and said, 'Maybe we did.'

'And I don't remember?'

Vanav shrugged, amused. She knew that he was only kidding.

'Wait, let me show you something,' Aarisha said. She made him sit by the little wall and went to the centre of the terrace. She struck a Kathak pose that she had learnt from her Kathak classes and danced for the next fifteen minutes.

There was a time when she had danced on this very terrace and he had watched her in awe. Once upon a time, she was a wish. Now, she was his reality. The journey he had traversed to reach from point A to point B had been an education in love. Against all hope.

Just as Vanav kissed her forehead, her phone rang; it was Soni. She answered the call to be told that her friends were waiting for her. Aarisha told her that she would be with them in ten minutes.

As Aarisha drove away in the car, Vanav heaved a sigh and called his mother.

'Hello ma, did you and papa reach safely? How is chachaji and everyone at home?'

As Vanav's mother started updating him about all the family gossip, he knew that this had been a close call. If he had not made a quick travel plan for his parents to go to his uncle's place in Bikaner, both Aarisha and his parents would have found out a side of him that he was sure neither could have handled. Not now, not ever.

15

'I need to tell you something.' It was Pragya on a video call with Aarisha.

'What is it? And where the hell are you?' Aarisha could hear a lot of noise.

'I eloped,' Pragya said.

'What? Are you serious?' Aarisha couldn't believe her bestie would do such a thing. Pragya panned her camera to her bags and also showed her that she was in a bus.

'Yes, I am. I myself didn't know that I could do this. What I'm sure of is that I don't see a life with anyone else except Nimish.'

'But you guys could have waited, right? What's the hurry?'

'I didn't tell you something. I overheard my dad and mom talking about fixing my marriage last month. My uncle brought this proposal from one of his friends' families. The guy is settled and all that shit. You know my parents. My sister was married at the age of twenty and I'm already twenty-two.'

'What did Nimish say?'

'He's ready to marry me. He got a promotion two months ago. We'll be a live-in couple for a few months until I get a job in Delhi. And then we'll probably get married.'

'His family?'

'They live in Mussoorie. He said he would convince them to accept me.'

'Are you sure about all this? Have you thought it through? I hope you know that there's no coming back from this.'

'A hundred times. Sometimes, all we need is to have some faith. And I'm as sure of Nimish as you're of Vanav,' said Pragya.

'Just take care. Let's meet during one of the weekends. Delhi and Udaipur aren't that far apart,' Aarisha said.

'Yes, let's meet. I'll keep you posted.'

'Please do.'

'If papa calls just tell him I haven't called you.'

Pragya reached the Kashmiri Gate bus stop in the evening. Nimish was waiting for her. Their excitement at seeing each other was mutually infectious. They took the metro and went to Hauz Khas where Nimish was staying alone. They dropped her bags off. As she checked his place out, she discovered that there were no basic provisions in the house. Not even tea or sugar.

'And someone said he has everything,' she taunted him, smiling.

With a naughty gleam in his eye, Nimish hugged her, kissed her cheek and said, 'I do have my everything.'

Pragya rubbed her nose against his. He kissed her and just when she thought it would lead to a bout of passionate lovemaking, she pushed him away.

'Patience, mister. First things first.'

'Then shall we do the most basic thing?' Nimish asked with a puppy-dog expression.

'Fuck you.'

The two decided to visit the closest departmental store to pick up some groceries.

While they were selecting the grocery items in the aisles and loading them into the shopping basket, Nimish was getting naughty with her. Every time they happened to be alone in an aisle, he would steal a kiss or pinch her waist. Pragya, enjoying it to the hilt, asked him to hold on to his horses until that night. As soon as they were done with their selection, she approached the cash counter. That was when she noticed Vanav. She stopped. And frowned. She withdrew a few paces so Vanav couldn't see her. Nimish nudged her enquiringly. Pragya gestured towards Vanav and told Nimish who he was. According to Aarisha, he ought to have been in Lucknow. As soon as Vanav paid for his purchases and left the store, Pragya moved into the check-out queue. She thought it was weird for Vanav to be in Delhi and that too in a departmental store picking up such a big load of groceries.

'Is he two-timing Aarisha?' Nimish asked.

'Too early to judge,' replied Pragya and decided to follow him. They dropped off their stuff at their apartment that was around the corner and hurried back. Vanav had just finished checking out and paying for his massive load of groceries. Nimish's bike tailed their quarry at a discreet distance to Panchsheel Park where Vanav finally parked his car. They watched him enter a house. Nimish parked his bike at the end of the lane from where they still had a clear view of the house.

Minutes later, Pragya saw Vanav step outside on to the balcony and lean against the balcony wall. A woman appeared at the doorway. She came outside a little, but then continued to hover at the balcony door.

'Oh fuck!' Pragya murmured and immediately messaged Aarisha:

DO YOU KNOW WHERE YOUR BOYFRIEND IS?

'It could just be a friend,' offered Nimish.

'I don't care. I only care about my friend. I know how much she loves him. And she should know where he is, even if he is with "just" a friend.'

The message was delivered to Aarisha. But it wasn't delivered to her alone. Vanav got the same message on his phone as well. Unbeknownst to Aarisha, her phone had spywares after the Dharamshala incident. He tracked all her chats. He had his reasons for doing so. Vanav moved into the house.

Three hours later, Aarisha read the message after the seminar she had been attending. She messaged back:

'HE'S WORKING IN LUCKNOW. WHY?'

Her message didn't get delivered. Aarisha continued with her hectic schedule for the day. Four hours later, Pragya's father telephoned Aarisha to find out if she knew where Pragya was.

Although Aarisha felt guilty to lie to him, she said she didn't know. She immediately telephoned Pragya. Once. Twice. Thrice. The rings went through all right, but the call wasn't picked up. When an anxious Aarisha called her for the fourth time, Vanav cut the call and messaged from Pragya's phone.

MAKING OUT WITH NIMISH. CALL YOU BACK SOON.

And then he looked at the charred bodies of both Pragya and Nimish.

Dead.

BOOK II
THE PAST

1

AJMER

Vanav was furious like never before. He knew his mother had packed, after a long time, his favourite lunch for school recess. He opened his tiffin box to find just one strand of the delicious Maggi noodles in the form of a smiley. It would have been better if someone had just eaten it all, but the prankster left that 'smiley' as a taunt and that was galling. Vanav knew exactly who the prankster was.

A few hours later, with hunger roaring inside him, he stood by a small lane, his bicycle parked by the side. This was the lane that his tormentor and target took every day to reach home at around this time. *Today, she'll get it from me*, he thought. As a girl swerved into the lane on her bicycle, Vanav almost leaped on to her.

'Binny *ki bachchi*! I won't spare you.'

She let go of her bicycle to scuffle with him. He could have hit her when she ruthlessly yanked his hair, but he didn't. Taking advantage of the fact that Vanav wouldn't ever strike her no matter how angry he was with her, Binny clawed him mercilessly and then pushed him away. While he tried to recover his balance, she scampered to her house at the end of the lane. The scratches hurt as Vanav ran behind her.

Binny and Vanav, being neighbours, had grown up together. As much as they were each other's best friend, they were each other's arch nemesis as well. Together, they were infamous in the entire locality as devils on the rampage. There was not a single sweet shop in the locality that had not been pranked for free delicacies. Their notoriety was such that, for some time now, whenever they popped into any of those shops, a peace offering of the day's special was given to each of them as *mooh dikhai*, or in other words, just for showing up. Although Binny was a year younger to Vanav, they behaved like contemporaries—so much so that the difference in their genders had also blurred. They never thought of themselves as boy and girl—only as a gang of two.

This wasn't the first time that Binny had hijacked Vanav's lunch. The last time around, she had been given a sound thrashing by her mother after Vanav had complained bitterly. But Binny had her reasons for her larceny. Why wouldn't Vanav share with her the jokes that he shared with his guy friends? This would seem like the silliest reason ever, but not for Binny. If her priority was Vanav, then his priority ought to be her and it was imperative that he be completely open with her. It got her goat to be excluded from his boys-only club. Whenever he shut her out, she would wonder, *Why? Am I too dumb to understand the joke?* And now she had found a way to avenge herself for the innumerable snubs.

Binny rushed home and commanded Mai-Ka-Lal, her pet dog, not to allow Vanav into the house. Mai-Ka-Lal was a stray that Binny had adopted as a pup. Over the years, Mai-Ka-Lal had turned into her fiercely loyal companion. When Vanav approached the threshold to Binny's house, Mai-Ka-Lal growled, bared her teeth menacingly and then let loose a volley of shrill barks at him. Vanav stopped at the door and hollered, 'I'll take care of you!' before he retreated from the furious canine, rubbing at the vicious scratches on his neck and arm. Both their bicycles still lay on their side on the road outside the house. Vanav punctured both the tyres of Binny's bicycle, picked up his own and rode home without a care in the world.

As soon as he got home, Vanav bathed and changed out of his clothes before applying anti-septic cream on the livid scratches. He had his meal and took a quick power nap. When he awoke, he cycled to his tuition class with his books.

At the tuition, it was the usual scene. Their mathematics teacher gave them some problems to solve and retreated inside to solve some problems that seemed to have his wife as a key component. Her squeals and moans made the boys snigger. One of the boys, a mischief-maker called Mayur, produced something from his pocket. The sniggers subsided into awed silence as they watched Mayur unfold the poster on the table. It was a centrefold from a *Playboy* magazine featuring a well-endowed nude. Their eyes bulged just looking at it, however Vanav felt too shy to even approach the table. The tittering started again. Vanav distanced himself slightly from the group.

'What's up with you?' Mayur asked, noticing Vanav's discomfort.

'It's someone's naked picture. What's there to giggle about?' Vanav retorted.

'Not someone. A nude girl. Why? Do you see a nude girl every day?' Mayur sneered while the others chortled. Vanav didn't know what more to say, so he remained silent.

Mayur teased him after the tuitions as well, but Vanav paid no heed to his baiting and rode home. His inner frustration at his inability to retaliate against Mayur transmogrified into a rant at his mother, Varsha Thakur, in the kitchen when he saw her preparing his most hated vegetable—bitter gourd—for dinner.

'Can't I have Maggi for dinner?' he carped.

'Maggi for breakfast, Maggi for lunch, Maggi for dinner. Get married to Maggi, why don't you?' snapped his exasperated mother. 'Now go and change. Papa wants to talk to you over dinner. Don't be late.'

Vanav pulled a face and took the stairs two at a time to his room. Under his breath, he cursed Binny, Mayur and the world at large. He dropped his trousers before going in for a shower and then froze. A sparkling nose stud bounded towards him from the other end of the room and now lay at his feet. Vanav whipped around, appalled to see a girl standing by his wardrobe. She was in full Indian bridal wear and looked as breath-taking as an incomplete symphony.

'Sorry to have commandeered your room like this,' she said softly.

'Who are you?' Vanav somehow managed to find his voice, yanking up his trousers in one swift movement.

'Daksh is your cousin, right?'

Vanav nodded.

'I'm his girlfriend. Aarisha Shergill. And trust me, I didn't see a thing!' she said the last part ineffectively suppressing gurgling laughter.

But Vanav did see *something*. Something he had never seen before in his life. Ever.

2

Vanav had to change and freshen up in his parents' bathroom, but not before he growled at his mother, for not warning him about the guest. For the first time in his life he had to vacate his room for someone else. A part of him was furious. But another part of him was . . . he couldn't quite define the feeling. As he bathed, her face rose before his eyes. And in such detail that he didn't realize that he had noticed so much in that brief encounter. The mole on the left side of her chin, the large greyish-blue eyes, the oval face, and then her voice ricocheted, *I'm his girlfriend*. Vanav turned off the faucet and quickly dried his hands, trying hard not to allow any risqué thoughts to enter his mind.

Ten minutes later, when he joined his father—Pratap Singh Thakur—he saw Daksh and Aarisha already seated at the table with him. She had changed into skinny jeans and a checked shirt.

'Meet Vanav Singh Thakur, my little cousin and the most intelligent person in our entire *khandaan* (dynasty),' said Daksh to Aarisha. She smiled at Vanav looking suitably impressed, not letting on that they had already met and in a far less formal setting.

'Nice to meet you, Vanav,' Aarisha stretched out her hand.

Only Vanav was aware of how much he was quaking in his shoes as he shook her long-fingered hand.

'Same here.'

'How much did you score last time?' Daksh asked.

'Ninety-nine per cent,' Vanav said, his face reddening.

'Damn! *Mamaji* (maternal uncle),' Daksh said glancing at Vanav's father, 'Mark my words! This boy will do us all proud one day.'

They continued with their dinner until Vanav's mother joined them and said, 'I think we should discuss the matter that has brought you here.' She looked alternately at her husband and Daksh before finally turning to Aarisha.

As the elders conversed, Vanav learnt that Aarisha Shergill studied with Daksh in his engineering college in Jalandhar. She belonged to a staunchly conservative family. She had kept her affair with Daksh a secret but one of her cousins had caught them making out in a cinema hall. The matter was promptly escalated to the elders who believed in only one diktat: a headstrong, hurly-burly hussy who had the cheek to clandestinely canoodle with a boy would have to be married off willy-nilly to the first alliance that came along. They soon found a suitable groom for her. When Daksh came to know about this impending doom, he hatched a plan, along with his batchmates, to elope with Aarisha on the day of her shotgun wedding. Everything went according to plan. He brought her to his uncle's home in Ajmer where he was sure nobody would even think of looking for them because Daksh's home was in Udaipur.

'What's the plan now? This can't be the solution,' Pratap interjected.

'I'm going home day after tomorrow. I'll have a talk with my father,' Daksh said, glancing at Aarisha. 'I don't think he or anyone from our family will have a problem.'

'Are you sure?' Pratap asked. He sounded doubtful, laced with a trace of contempt; he didn't seem to have a high opinion of Daksh's father's broad-mindedness. It made Aarisha glance at Daksh. He took a few seconds to respond.

'I am.'

He paused thoughtfully before adding, 'Once I've had a talk with *papaji*, I'll contact her parents and let them know that she is with me and that we want to get married. If they agree we do so with them as witnesses . . . else . . .' he trailed off looking around, then added a question, 'Until they let me know their opinion about this, can Aarisha stay here, please? I request you.'

'That's not an issue. She can stay in Vanav's room. And he can move in with us. Daksh, you can sleep on the couch in the living room,' said Pratap firmly.

'The storeroom is fine for me,' Vanav butted in realizing perhaps that was what his father wanted to talk to him about. Daksh gave him a smile.

'No police will be involved, right?' Mrs Thakur asked.

'Don't worry *maamiji* (auntie). They can involve the police if they want to but . . .'

'We're both adults,' said Aarisha in her soft voice. 'Even if my family were to tell the police that Daksh kidnapped me, I will tell them that I came here voluntarily.'

As she spoke, Vanav keenly observed her. The way her shapely lips moved prettily as she spoke. He counted the number of times she ran her right hand through her silky hair, the number of times she blinked and even the number of times she chewed her food before swallowing. He noticed that she, unusually, used her left hand to eat her food. As she ate a tad slowly, she kept apologizing to the others at the table. At one point, he noticed a grain of rice stuck to the side of her lower lip—he wanted to tell her about it but didn't. There was something imperfect in all the perfection she exuded—and Vanav found that mysterious imperfection fascinating.

'Take your time, beta,' Pratap Singh said, finishing with his dinner. 'Excuse me. *Kaun Banega Crorepati* (*KBC*) is about to start.' He rose and left the dining space.

'Nothing and nobody can come between your mamaji and *KBC*. Anyway, how did you two meet? In college?' Mrs Thakur asked with the avid curiosity of the typical gossip monger, even though she knew perfectly well that they had met in college, because Daksh had told her. As Daksh started narrating, with Aarisha interjecting now and then, Vanav simply sat there admiring her. Nothing of what she said registered but everything else—her mannerisms, her short laughs, smirks, everything—were fast getting imprinted on his mind.

After Mrs Thakur felt satisfied that she had all the details of their love story, she let Daksh and Aarisha go up to Vanav's room for a talk while she joined her husband for her favourite *saans-bahu* serial.

It took Vanav a few minutes to shift all his important stuff and bits and pieces to the storeroom, which happened to have an extra bed. He was about to doze off when his mother came to him and asked him to go upstairs and check if the two would like to have glasses of hot milk before turning in. He went up to the terrace through the backdoor of his room as that was the shorter route—and stopped by the terrace doorway. Aarisha and Daksh were in the distance, standing by the cemented water tank and talking, their hands clasped.

'Why can't I go with you to your place?' Aarisha asked Daksh sotto voce.

'Let me first have a talk with *papaji*. I feel it would be better for me to do it alone, I can't explain why.'

Aarisha was about to say something when she sensed a presence.

'Excuse me,' Vanav cleared his throat. Aarisha jerked her hand out of Daksh's clasp.

'What are you doing here, brother?' Daksh asked.

'Ma wanted to know if you two wanted to have milk before you went to bed,' Vanav said.

'No. But thanks,' Aarisha said.

Vanav turned to leave when Daksh stopped him.

'Brother, can you please stay in your room for a little while? If uncle or auntie come up, just call out to me immediately. Remember, don't come out on to the terrace, just call out.'

'All right,' Vanav said.

'Also, if they ask, tell them that we three plan to chit chat all through the night. We aren't planning to sleep.'

'Okay,' Vanav replied and went inside.

'Why did you have to tell him all that?' Aarisha chided and was about to say more when Daksh pressed his lips to hers, picked her up in his strong arms and bore her away to the shadowed area by the water tank.

Inside his room, Vanav stubbed his toe on something small as he walked to his bed. He looked down. It was the same nose stud that had rolled over to him. *Why didn't she retrieve it?* he wondered. He picked it up and gazed at it for a while before suddenly kissing it tenderly. Deeply embarrassed by this foolishness, he glanced around furtively. When his mother came calling, he relayed what Daksh had asked him to say. That the three would spend the night chit-chatting. Vanav didn't realize when he dozed off clutching the nose stud while Daksh and Aarisha continued to make love into the wee hours.

3

Vanav was surprised to see two tiffin boxes inside his bag when he opened it during recess. One had *mirchi ka achaar* and a couple of aloo parathas. When he opened the other box, the aroma of Maggi noodles filled his nostrils. *Why would ma give me two boxes?* That was when Binny crept up behind him.

'I'm sorry, Vanav,' she said. 'You can't stop talking to me just because I ate your Maggi.'

Vanav looked at her for a moment and then chuckled. He handed over his aloo parathas to Binny and also shared the noodles with her.

'Binny, have you ever felt weird at your first sight of someone, a total stranger?' he asked in a muffled voice, stuffing his face with food.

'Weird how?'

'Like you see someone for the first time and feel things that you've never felt before,' Vanav did his best to explain the phenomenon.

Binny looked baffled. 'I've no idea what you're talking about. Did you see a ghost?'

Vanav realized that he was incapable of articulating his experience—nor was her understanding lofty enough to grasp his meaning.

'Yes,' he conceded unhappily.

'Oh wow! I've always wanted to see a ghost. What was he like?' Binny was ecstatic.

'Not he. She. And she looked exactly like you!' Vanav polished off the last strand of the noodles and nimbly leaped out of her reach to run towards the classroom.

'Vanav, *kutte*, I will put rat poison into your Maggi the next time!' she tore after him.

Later that day, when Vanav returned home from school, no one answered the doorbell. He opened the door with the spare key that was always kept in the secret place known only to the family. As he stepped in, he heard sounds from the terrace. Curious, he went up to his room and the strains of a Rajasthani folk song playing on the stereo grew louder. He followed the song and went up to the terrace where he saw Aarisha dancing to the song with ghungroos around her ankles. He quietly let his bag drop to the floor and sat down, rivetted, oblivious to everything but her exquisitely graceful movements. He wasn't aware of the beatific smile of awe on his face. He blinked only when she stopped after the song had ended.

'When did you come?' Aarisha was panting softly, genuinely surprised to see him. She turned off the stereo and wiped the perspiration that beaded her brow with a dainty hand towel.

Vanav stood frozen, feeling incredibly tongue-tied.

'I'm sorry, I came about five minutes ago and was spellbound by your dance. I couldn't help but sit and watch. I hope you don't mind.'

'Oh, don't be sorry. It's absolutely fine,' she said airily and sat down cross-legged to untie her ghungroos. She noticed him staring at her ghungroo set.

'D'you recognize this dance form?' she asked.

Vanav shook his head in ignorance.

'It's Kathak. I'm a trained Kathak dancer,' she said smiling proudly.

'You dance like a queen!' Vanav blurted out involuntarily.

Aarisha burst out laughing. 'A queen?'

'Yes. A queen . . . *Ranisa*.'

'But I'm sure queens don't dance like this,' she said, having successfully unlaced the ghungroo from around one ankle.

My queen does, Vanav thought, but said, 'May I please call you Ranisa?'

Aarisha glanced at him, their gazes interlocking for a trice. She smiled and nodded. 'May I make a request?' she asked taking both the anklets in her hand and rising.

'Anything,' Vanav said fervently. She handed over the jingling anklets to him. Vanav stood confused.

'The thing is, I love to dance but your Daksh *bhaiya* doesn't like it. That's why I did this today when I was home alone. If he sees these with me, he may not like it. Although I can keep them with me, I am worried that if I do, I'll be tempted to dance again. So, please keep them with you. I'll take them from you if I ever need them.'

'Sure!' said Vanav with alacrity.

Aarisha thanked him and then seemed lost in thought for a moment. Then she said, 'I too have a name for you.'

Vanav looked up at her expectantly, his face aglow.

'Thakur sahab.'

Vanav tried in vain to control the crimson tide that spread over his face, 'I'll keep these safe.'

He left the terrace but returned almost immediately.

'What is it?' Aarisha asked.

'If you love dancing then why do you avoid it just because bhaiya doesn't like it?'

With a thoughtful gaze, Aarisha said, 'A little sacrifice adds life to one's love story.'

Vanav lapped this up, looking deep into her eyes.

He came down to his makeshift room, went to his study table and opened the bottom drawer in which he kept all his prized possessions. It had his academic certificates and his medals from the various Olympiads and inter-school competitions. More importantly, it had the nose stud. He tenderly placed the ghungroo in the drawer. But before he put them in, he gently touched them to his forehead—as if he had seen a spark of the divine in them.

It was late in the evening when Daksh returned home with his uncle and aunt. The next morning, he was to travel to Udaipur. After dinner, Pratap went to watch *KBC*, Mrs Thakur tidied the kitchen and sent Vanav to find out whether Aarisha or Daksh wanted hot milk before their bedtime.

Vanav went up to the terrace. It was dark, but as Vanav's pupils adjusted themselves to the tenebrosity, he could see Daksh smooching Aarisha passionately. He froze by the terrace's entrance.

'Slowly, Daksh. Go slow. There's no need to hurry, I am not going anywhere!' Vanav heard Aarisha say.

Daksh undid the string fastening of her salwar trousers and tugged on it. He positioned himself between her thighs. She wrapped her legs around his hips. A second later, a moan escaped her. Vanav could make out the silhouette of each of Daksh's thrusts.

'I love you, Daksh,' Aarisha mouthed.

'I love you, Aarisha,' Daksh responded.

His hands were on her breasts above her kameez. To Vanav it seemed as if each thrust was timed with his heartbeat. He heard Aarisha ask for more and more and more, until Daksh eventually stopped moving and held her tight. They were still once again. Vanav turned away and stole quietly and quickly back to the storeroom downstairs. He didn't switch on the lights.

A few minutes later his mother entered the room, yawning. She casually switched on the lights.

'Do they want milk or not?' she asked and then shrieked.

A compass had pierced Vanav's palm through and through and his hand was soaked in blood. Vanav gazed at his mother, his eyes glazed. As if he didn't know why his mother shrieked.

4

'How did this happen?' Mrs Thakur's scream had alarmed the entire household and his father was in the room in a flash. The next minute, Daksh and Aarisha rushed in.

'It . . . it was dark, and I accidently put my hand on it,' Vanav stuttered, hoping against hope that this was a plausible explanation. As his mother ran for the first-aid kit, Aarisha came forward and took his hand in a firm grasp. Daksh and Pratap hovered anxiously over him as they waited for the casualty's mother to hurry back with the medical supplies.

'Just look at me,' commanded Aarisha, gripping Vanav's hand. 'You'll be all right.' She spoke like an expert at medical crises: 'Daksh, soak some Dettol in a cotton swab.'

Daksh did as he was told.

'On the count of three, I'll pull the compass out, okay?' she looked at Vanav, who nodded wordlessly. As she drew the compass out in one swift motion, his body stiffened for a moment, but no sound betrayed him.

'I must say you're a very brave boy,' Aarisha said encouragingly as she put the bloodied compass away and dabbed at the bleeding wound with the Dettol-soaked cotton wad. The antiseptic burned against his skin but Vanav couldn't stop looking at Aarisha. And then, with some effort, he averted his eyes to look at his wound.

After bandaging the wound properly, everyone left the room, instructing Vanav not to study that night. Mrs Thakur couldn't thank Aarisha enough.

'It's okay, auntie. I'm the "doctor" in my house. I learnt all this from my grandad,' she laughed.

'I wish these two were my parents. After this incident, they would have been highly impressed with their future daughter-in-law,' Daksh joked, whispering in her ears as they stepped out of the room.

That night, Vanav couldn't sleep. There was an inexplicable unease which he couldn't ignore. Every time he tried to picture Aarisha's smiling face, it was superimposed by the heaving eroticism of the dark passion that he had witnessed on the terrace. It sullied the purity of her ethereal beauty. *Why does it bother me so?* Aarisha and Daksh were a couple. They were doing what any couple would do. So, why did it disturb him like this? He had never been in a relationship—never touched, or been touched by, a girl in a sexual way. But he wasn't a fool. He knew what people in love did. Unable to bear it anymore, he went into the bathroom and dunked an entire bucket of icy cold water on himself hoping to derail his train of thought. As he lay on his bed shivering, he stared at his bandaged hand. She had nursed it. Vanav pressed the centre of his bandaged palm until a little blood spurted out of wound. He smiled—in the pain he felt her presence within him.

The next morning, Daksh left for Udaipur. As Vanav was getting ready to leave for school, he was surprised to see Aarisha struggling with his father's old scooter.

'That doesn't work,' he said, but Aarisha determinedly continued, trying to kick-start the bucket of bolts.

'Vanav beta, your tiffin is ready,' his mother called out.

Vanav went in and asked his mother, 'What's she doing with papa's scooter?'

'She is such a darling,' his mother replied. 'I was supposed to go to the market to fetch a few things, but she offered to run the errand for me. She wants to stay here, not as a guest, but as family. God bless her. Daksh is really lucky.'

Vanav grabbed his tiffin box and ran out. As he hitched his bag to his bicycle, he heard the scooter's engine sputter into life. He turned to see Aarisha astride on the scooter.

'Everything works,' she yelled out over the noise of the revving engine, 'you just need to know how to make it work.' Aarisha buckled on an old helmet and said, 'Hop on, I'll drop you off.'

'No, it's okay,' refused Vanav hurriedly.

By then his mother emerged from the house, 'She's right. You're hurt, so spare the bicycle today and go with her.'

Vanav sat pillion with his bag slung over his shoulder. No words were exchanged and Vanav was extra careful not to touch her. He had gooseflesh all through the drive and the only time he opened his mouth was to give directions.

'How's your hand?' she asked.

'It doesn't hurt any more,' he lied blatantly.

'Good.'

For the entire journey, he kept shifting his eyes from the left rear-view mirror to the right, stealing glances of her. *How amazing would it be if we never arrived at school*, he thought—if only these roads could stretch on infinitely, the fuel in the scooter could last forever and he could remain in the pillion seat and give her directions until the end of time.

'When do I pick you up?' she asked as they reached his school.

'I'll come back by myself, thanks,' he said.

'Okay,' she flashed a smile and zoomed off.

The boys who saw Aarisha dropping Vanav were consumed with curiosity about her, while Binny was the only one who noticed his bandaged hand rather than the vision of loveliness that had driven him to school.

'I told you not to hit me. See, God has cursed you,' she said with her infuriatingly smart-ass smugness.

'Shut up, Binny!' Vanav retorted.

'But how did this happen?'

Before Vanav could answer, Mayur and the other boys came to him and inquired about the girl on the scooter.

'Who's she?'

'My cousin's girlfriend. Why?' Vanav asked, reading the lust in their eyes.

'She rides so well!' Mayur said. The other boys chortled at the double-entendre. Vanav side-stepped them and went into the school building while Binny trailed after him asking belatedly about the person who had given him a lift to school.

Later that day, during their tuition class, the other boys sniggered among themselves when their teacher went inside his house upon being summoned petulantly by his over-sexed wife. Mayur took out an overused novel whose pages were coming loose from its spine. The author's name, however, could be clearly read: Mastram. Vanav knew who Mastram was: the daddy of Hindi porn literature. Mayur started reading out a descriptive passage from the book describing a couple having sex, substituting Aarisha with the name of the female character. Vanav snatched the book from Mayur's hands and saw that the name of the character in the book was Khushboo. But that name was scored out and Aarisha's scribbled over it. Mayur demanded the book back, but Vanav ripped out the pages before flinging it to the floor, wondering how they had discovered Aarisha's name. The teacher returned to the classroom, bellowed at the unruly boys and resumed the tuition. As soon as the class was over, Mayur and Vanav started to fight outside the tuition teacher's house. The other boys intervened promptly and broke it up.

'You shouldn't fight with shitty people,' chided Binny when they were cycling back home, he riding pillion on hers. She then volunteered to tell him how Mayur had wheedled Aarisha's name out of her to solve Vanav's mystery. Vanav fell silent the rest of the way home.

At night, when his mother sent him to Aarisha's room upstairs to ask if she needed anything before she hit the sack, he once again did not find her in the room. Curious, he went to the terrace and noticed that she was lying on top of the water tank. He called out to her, but she didn't respond. If something was amiss, he climbed to the top of the tank. He was about to shake her when he saw her face illuminated brightly in the silvery moonlight. For some time, he gazed at her incredible beauty. Then he noticed her cleavage was a little too visible as her *dupatta* had slipped away from her bosom. He draped the silken material over her properly to restore her maidenly virtue. Her hand shifted, and he saw a bottle of Coke. With a frown he sniffed at the bottle and realized that there was a strong smell emanating from it. Vanav was about to take a sip when Aarisha made a faint noise. He leaned forward.

'I love you, Daksh,' she pulled him down, murmuring drunkenly.

Vanav immediately extricated himself and ran down and informed his mother that Aarisha was already asleep. Once again at midnight, he emptied a bucket of icy cold water over himself and after he picked the scab over his healing wound, inflicting agony on himself and making it bleed afresh, he fell asleep with a satisfied smile.

Aarisha wanted to drop Vanav to school the next day, but he left early on his bicycle, long before she could get ready. On the way to school, he bought an Amul powder tin box. He had already stolen a matchbox and some oil from the kitchen before leaving. When he reached school, it didn't take him long to find Mayur and the gang.

'Sorry about yesterday,' said Vanav, holding out the tin box by its edges and adding, 'Here are some sweets for you.'

Mayur's eyes lit up as he excitedly put his hand into the metal box and then howled with agony, jerking his hand away from the hot oil inside the box.

'Never again talk shit about Aarisha!' Vanav tossed the tin box away and walked off.

5

The principal summoned Vanav's father for a meeting, so the next morning, Pratap told him to come to school with him on his scooter and leave his bicycle behind. Vanav sensed that something was wrong.

'How can he be so violent?' The principal raged at Pratap Thakur after recounting the previous day's incident. Pratap was visibly embarrassed and at a loss as to how to answer the question because this was the first time he'd received a complaint about Vanav. Truth be told, even Pratap was surprised to learn that Vanav had burnt Mayur's hand.

'Did you do it?' Pratap asked Vanav. The latter was standing beside him with his head hanging low. Mayur and his parents were sitting adjacent to his father. Vanav only nodded a 'yes'.

'Why?' Pratap asked. Vanav remained silent.

'Why did he do it?' the principal asked Mayur.

'I don't know. He said there were sweets inside the box. And when I dipped my hand, I realized it had hot oil,' Mayur replied, avoiding Vanav's fulminating eye.

'So, it was just a silly prank?' said the principal looking at Vanav.

'Do you know how harmful this prank of yours was? I want you to apologize to Mayur first.'

'I'm sorry,' said Vanav softly.

'Only because Vanav is academically brilliant am I letting him go this time with just a warning. Otherwise, I would have suspended him,' the principal told Pratap and closed the matter.

Vanav followed Pratap outside. The way Pratap started his scooter with an angry kick told Vanav that it was better not to talk. He remained quiet all through the day at school. Mayur and the gang shot him funny glances, but he didn't react. Binny kept pestering him to tell her why he was so quiet, but Vanav didn't respond.

'Is there anything you want to share, beta?' his mother asked when he returned from tuitions. Vanav said 'no', went into the storeroom and locked himself in. It was only when Aarisha knocked softly and asked him to come for dinner that he emerged.

'Dinner is ready. What are you doing?' she asked.

'I am studying,' Vanav lied. All he had done was make sketches of Aarisha's face. Nobody but Binny knew that he was quite the budding artist. Once done, he kept staring at the sketches until he heard the knock on the door again.

'We're waiting for you. Eat first and then study,' she said.

'I'll be there in a minute,' Vanav called from inside.

Aarisha went away. Vanav, picked up the sketches and shredded them into tiny pieces so that nobody would ever know. He deposited half the paper scraps in the dustbin in his room and the other half in the kitchen bin.

When he joined his parents and Aarisha, he sensed the tense atmosphere at the dining table.

'Did anyone from your family call you?' Vanav's mother asked Aarisha.

She took the bowl from her and said, 'I did get a few messages from my brother, but I'm yet to respond. Daksh asked me to keep the phone switched off for as long as possible.'

'They can track the phone, can't they?' Mrs Thakur said adding, 'I saw this on *Crime Patrol*.'

'Not the phone. The sim card can be tracked,' Vanav volunteered.

'Even if they do so, it's all right. I've done nothing wrong. Nor has Daksh.'

Nobody said a word after that.

When Vanav retired to his room, he sensed someone standing by the door. He turned around and a smile escaped him.

'Ranisa!' he exclaimed.

'Why did you injure that friend of yours?'

'Which friend?' he asked although he knew exactly whom she meant.

'Auntie told me. What happened?' Aarisha stepped inside and sat on the bed. Vanav remained standing by his study table.

'He deserved to be injured.'

'What did he do?'

Vanav was quiet. He looked anywhere but at her.

'I can see that you don't want to share it with me.'

'Nothing like that. He said shitty things about someone.'

'About whom?'

'Someone I . . . I . . .' Vanav struggled for the right word.

'Love?'

For the first time, he looked at her. Those greyish-blue eyes. All his life's secrets were trapped in them. And the purpose of his life, Vanav felt, was to unravel them one by one.

'I don't know,' he said slowly and added, 'I just can't handle it if someone talks shit about her.'

'Her? Hmm, it's a girl. I guessed that,' Aarisha said, looking amused. There was a hint of a blush on Vanav's face.

'Anger isn't good, Vanav. Just take it easy. By the way, does she know that you . . .?' she chose her words wisely and said, '. . . can't take shit about her from anyone?'

'How will she ever know?'

'Aren't you planning to tell her?'

Vanav shook his head and then took few seconds before he replied, 'When we pray, we just *know* the prayer will reach God. We don't have to do anything but to pray with all our heart and soul, isn't it, Ranisa?'

'Do you realize you're a little too intense for your age? I wish your Daksh bhaiya was also like this.'

Vanav stood there with a I-don't-know look.

'And I love it when you call me Ranisa. Nobody has ever called me that,' Aarisha said with a smile.

'Thank you,' Vanav flashed an unsure smile back.

'Vanav! Come out, right now!' It was Pratap bellowing from the drawing room. It was evident that he was furious. Aarisha and Vanav had a momentary eye lock before he ran out of the room. Aarisha followed him.

6

Aarisha had never seen anyone looking as furious as Pratap seemed at that moment. He looked like he could wring Vanav's scrawny neck.

'Go upstairs, Aarisha,' he snapped and looked at his wife meaningfully. Mrs Thakur took Aarisha's arm and gently coaxed her up the stairs.

As soon as the ladies had left the room, Pratap turned to Vanav, 'Somaniji found this bottle behind our house,' Pratap said, dangling the incriminating evidence, a Coke bottle, before Vanav's alarmed face. The Somanis lived next door.

'I don't think I need to tell you why he brought this bottle to me!'

Vanav was silent.

'Did you bring alcohol home?' Pratap's tone was fierce. A few seconds later, Vanav nodded a 'yes'.

'I don't believe this. What has happened to you? First that dangerous prank and now this? How dare you bring alcohol inside the house or even think of touching it?' Pratap roared and slapped Vanav so hard across his cheek that the boy tottered back a few steps to stay upright.

'Do I need to sit with you every single day and tell you why it's wrong?' Another slap with just as much force as the first met Vanav's terrified face and he nearly lost his balance. Vanav shook his head quietly as if to say 'no'.

'Then why did you do it? Who's teaching you all this?' Each question was punctuated with an infuriated slap. 'If I find you indulging in such activities again, I warn you . . .!' he slapped him even harder the final time.

Vanav stood his ground.

'Now get lost,' Pratap snapped.

Vanav turned to leave. He stopped. Turned around. 'I'm sorry, papaji. It won't happen again,' he murmured.

Pratap raised his voice to summon his wife—and retired to his room.

Vanav remained seated at his study table in his make-shift room ever since he had come in a few hours ago. Only the table light on his study table was switched on. It was very late. He heard a soft knock on the door. He opened the door. A smile flashed across his face.

'Ranisa!' he said.

Aarisha laid a finger on her lips, hushing him as she came in, and closed the door behind her. Holding Vanav's hand, she led him to the bed and sat him down, while she sat on the chair that he had just vacated.

'What happened? Did uncle beat you?' Aarisha's eyes were on his.

'Let me switch on the light,' he stood up. Aarisha made him sit down again.

'It's okay. I asked you something.'

'Yeah. He did.'

'Why? Auntie says he has never hit you before.'

'Perhaps I gave him a reason to do so.'

'What did you do now?'

Vanav averted his eyes, 'There was something . . .'

'Look at me,' she commanded. He obeyed. And knew he could never lie looking into those eyes.

'The Coke bottle that you had thrown from the terrace. Our neighbour found it and understood what it had contained. Papaji thought it was mine.'

Aarisha face-palmed herself with guilt. 'All because of me,' she moaned. 'I shouldn't have chucked it there, what was I thinking!'

'What was in it?'

'Rum. Old Monk.' She removed her hand from her face and said, 'I'm so sorry.'

'Don't be sorry,' Vanav said. *I didn't mind the slaps*, he thought.

'Why not? You can slap me and avenge yourself,' Aarisha said raising his hand to her cheek. Vanav instantly jerked his hand away.

'Ranisa, please.'

'Your Daksh bhaiya would have slapped me.'

'Well, I'm not Daksh bhaiya.'

'I know. You don't seem like someone who can hit anyone. But I'm really sorry.'

Vanav gave her a quiet smile with an intense look.

'I think you'll be one helluva desirable dude in a few years from now. You have that thing in your eyes.'

'What thing?'

'That thing which is the perfect bait for every girl's emotions.'

Feeling slightly awkward, Vanav decided to digress.

'Don't you miss your parents, Ranisa?'

Aarisha twirled away on the swivel chair. With her back to him she remained quiet for some time. When she eventually spoke, he could sense her voice was choked with remorse, 'I miss them. A lot. Especially papa. He was always very proud of me and never discouraged me from doing anything. He was coercing me into getting married urgently only because he was under heavy pressure from the other members of my family. I'm sure he would have never forced me to do anything against my will. I know I've compromised his position in the family by eloping.'

Vanav didn't know whether he should speak up or not.

'Now . . . as soon as Daksh and I get married, I'll go right back and apologize to him. I'm sure that when he sees my choice everything will be all right.'

'I'm sure,' Vanav agreed. She was casually examining his stuff on the study table.

'So, this is where the genius of the family shapes up,' she flipped open his books and diaries.

Vanav couldn't hold back his smile.

'Tomorrow, I'll treat you to your favourite thing. Tell me what you like.'

Vanav thought for a few moments and then said, 'Perhaps a *kachoda* or some *saakhe* with *kadi*. But it's really not necessary.'

'You know what they say?'

'What?'

'When you take pain for someone, you start belonging to that person. So, you have to obey me.'

Vanav took a few seconds to respond, 'As you say Ranisa,' he conceded.

'By the way, what's a kachoda? Big brother of kachodi?' she giggled endearingly.

'Perhaps someone who is in love with kachodi. You'll know tomorrow.'

'Yeah right. Anyway, sleep now. I'm off,' Aarisha said. She stopped at the door and turned around, 'Tell me something, Thakur sahab. You got a good pasting from your father through no fault of your own but for something that I had done. Didn't you feel like telling me not to drink?'

'I think we do what we feel like doing. If you want to drink, who am I to stop you? But yes, whenever you drink, I'll make sure the bottle disappears without a trace from now on.'

Aarisha smiled, 'You're quite mature for your age. Goodnight, Thakur sahab.'

'Good night, Ranisa.'

As the door clicked shut behind her, Vanav drew the table lamp and mirror close to his face and examined the red weals left behind by the slaps.

When you take pain for someone, you start belonging to that person. Vanav beamed from ear to ear.

7

Vanav was in the shower when Binny arrived. She stood outside the bathroom door, chivvying and harrying him to hurry up. He discovered that the urgency was no urgency at all; she just wanted to hang out. Aimlessly roaming the streets on a weekend and eating chaat at the expense of Vanav's pocket money was Binny's favourite leisure time activity.

Another pastime was to keep a beady eye on Vanav and report anything even remotely suspicious to his mother. The very idea of Vanav being harangued by his mother because of her snitching tickled her pink. Binny hadn't been over to Vanav's for a few days now—the longest she'd been away. When she came in, Mrs Thakur told her that he was now in the storeroom because a guest was occupying his room. Binny stormed into his makeshift bedroom and started inspecting every nook and corner of it until she discovered the ghungroos in the bottom drawer of Vanav's study table. She was holding this in her hand when the bathroom door opened.

'Are you turning into a girl?' Binny sneered.

'*Binny ki bachchi*, put that back, now!' roared Vanav.

She immediately realized that the ghungroos were way more important to him than she had originally assumed.

'This goes to auntie, now!' she roared back.

'If you leave the room with that, I swear I'll kill you,' Vanav said trying to grab her.

'If you come any closer, I'll scream,' warned Binny with unholy glee at having touched a raw nerve.

'Don't!'

'Okay. I want you to kneel here and confess that I'm way better than you.'

Vanav pulled a wry face and knelt, 'You are way better than me,' he said obediently.

Binny was taken aback at his instant capitulation. She gave the ghungroos to him.

'What has happened to you? You never give in so easily.'

Vanav took the ghungroos from her and replaced it in the bottom drawer of his study table.

'Binny, I don't mind if you take everything from me. Please don't touch these again.'

Binny received his message loud and clear. But what confused her was that a pair of ghungroos (of all things) had suddenly taken on such a disproportionate importance to Vanav. Weird!

'You ready?' It was Aarisha who had wandered into Vanav's room now.

Binny had vaguely seen her once, when she had dropped Vanav to school.

'Hi, I'm Binny. And you must be Aarisha,' Binny said.

'Hi Binny. Yes, I'm Aarisha,' she said and then, turning towards Vanav she asked, 'Is she the . . .'

'No. No!' Vanav hurriedly interrupted her, 'Binny and I are childhood friends.'

'That's cute. Then why can't she join us?' Aarisha invited.

Vanav glanced at Binny, hoping she would say no.

'I think I should definitely come with you guys. But where are you going?' Binny asked.

Vanav knew his flight of fancy of being with Aarisha alone had just crash-landed.

'I was taking him out for a treat. You can come along too,' Aarisha said.

Within the next half hour, the three were at Shankar Chaat at Gol Pyau, Naya Bazaar. Aarisha took both of them on Pratap's scooter with Binny perched in the middle. Aarisha had given Vanav the cash. He brought them kachoda first and then saakhe with kadi.

As Aarisha and Binny chatted desultorily, enjoying the al fresco treat, Vanav noticed a couple of guys lounging by the chaat shop, eyeing Aarisha lecherously. It made him deeply uncomfortable. Instead of listening to the girls' conversation, his attention was focussed on these lotharios. Vanav subtly stepped sideways and blocked their line of view, almost as if he were guarding Aarisha, who was oblivious to his manoeuvre. The voyeurs shifted their position and continued to ogle the beautiful girl and Vanav jockeyed in again, obstructing their view.

'What's wrong with you?' Binny carped. 'Why are you so antsy? Has someone dropped ice down your trousers?' she laughed inordinately at her own wit. Aarisha joined in.

'Are you both done?' Vanav asked.

'Yes,' they chorused.

'Dargah Sharif is only a kilometre away. Why don't you guys go on ahead and wait for me at the gate?'

'And why aren't you coming with us?' Aarisha asked.

'I'm telling you, he'll have more kachodas,' Binny assured Aarisha.

'Shut up. I need to pee,' said Vanav, 'I'll join you guys by the time you get there,' he looked quite convincing.

'Come on, Binny, let's go,' Aarisha kick-started the scooter. Binny perched on the pillion.

'Don't be late, Thakur sahab,' Aarisha threw a glance over her shoulder, making eye contact with Vanav.

'I'll be there soon, Ranisa,' he promised without looking away. Their nicknames for each other suggested a rapport that somehow excluded Binny and left her feeling she was out in the cold.

As soon as the girls left, Vanav checked to see where the two voyeurs were. They were still having their chaat. Vanav looked around and espied a grocer. He quickly went into the shop and asked for two transparent plastic bags. The shop owner knew Pratap and recognized Vanav. He smilingly complied with the lad's request and handed over the packets.

Vanav crossed over to the open gutter by the road. He squatted and collected the filthy sewage water in the two plastic packets and packed them tight like water-balloons. As he stood up, he noticed the scopophilias getting on to a flashy motorbike. Vanav masked his face with his handkerchief and briskly walked towards them. The moment the guy started his bike, a plastic packet exploded in his face, spilling its malodorous contents over his hair and clothes. Before he knew it, another stink bomb landed on the pillion rider. The air turned blue with their fluent imprecations as they hurriedly mopped at their faces and clothes. A few kind people rushed over to help them, but nobody could point out the culprit as Vanav had darted off into a side lane by then and was well on his way to Dargah Sharif. He had promised Aarisha that he would be there soon.

Vanav was more than happy to be Aarisha's guide inside the Dargah. The vibe of the place took her by surprise. She could feel divinity in the air. When Vanav told her that whoever made an earnest wish at the Dargah had their wish granted, Aarisha immediately wanted to try it out. She urged Binny and Vanav to also make their wishes. There was a long, winding queue, but before Binny could decide what she should wish for, she was nudged forward by the ushers minding the queue. Aarisha wished that both Daksh's family and her own would accept them. When Vanav saw Aarisha fervently make her wish with her eyes squeezed shut, he couldn't think of anything to wish for, his mind went blank. He knew he couldn't wish for what he truly desired—that would be very wrong. So, he waited for Aarisha to open her eyes and trailed along after her. He then conducted the girls to the famous sweet shops by the Dargah where they ate mouth-watering *sohan halwa* and Vanav stayed vigilant for roadside romeos.

In the evening, on his way back from his tuition, he pondered on why it bothered him so much when others looked at Aarisha. He had never felt like this before. The answer came to him out of the blue: it was because those satyrs didn't perceive her the way he did. And then he asked himself: did lust and love go hand in hand? Were sex and lust the only plausible connection between a man and a woman? The fact that he couldn't answer this question disappointed him. The more he struggled with the conundrum, the more he realized the depths of his ignorance on the subject. The more aware he became of his naiveté and the more convinced he grew that perhaps sex was indeed the only viable relationship between a man and a woman. He wasn't fully satisfied, however, with his reasoning.

As Vanav cycled past a wine shop, he stopped. One look at the shop and a happy smile appeared on his face. Aarisha had treated him with his favourite chaat. It was time for a return gift. He checked his pockets. He had a total of Rs 325 left from his savings. He parked his bicycle outside the shop and wandered in.

'And when did Pratapji start drinking?' the vintner joked merrily when Vanav asked for a bottle of rum.

'From today. Also, give me a bottle of Coke.'

He was given a bottle of Old Monk and a bottle of Coke, both of which Vanav carefully stowed in his bag. He planned to mix the two and discard the rum bottle before entering his house. Just as Vanav was preparing to leave, he heard someone call him. Three men stood at the street corner; they had a hooligan vibe to them. They showed him a printout of a girl's face. Aarisha's.

'Have you seen this girl anywhere?' one of them asked him. Vanav shook his head, 'no'. He realized that these must be men deployed by her family to hunt her down. If they had made it all the way to Ajmer, they would find their way to their house soon enough. As his mind busily computed his next course of action, he heard one of the men say, '*Kutiya saali, pata nahi kahan jaake marr gayi hai.*'

He didn't hear anything beyond the word 'kutiya'. He immediately turned to the men and said, 'I think I know where she is.'

The three thugs looked up.

8

Vanav was having breakfast. Pratap was reading the Hindi newspaper at the breakfast table and absently having his breakfast. There was a small news article on the fifth page that caught Vanav's eye. *Three men were recovered from an abandoned house with third-degree burns.* Vanav read the news item with a blank expression although his mind recollected every detail of the incident.

After he told the men that he knew where the girl was, the men wanted to know more details; he told them that he had seen someone resembling the girl meet a boy at 10 p.m. a few times, at an abandoned godown three lanes away from his house. Vanav was familiar with it because it happened to be one of his and Binny's favourite haunts. The godown went to rack and ruin after the family that owned both it and the house adjacent to it died in a tragic accident. Vanav asked the men to wait inside the godown around 10 p.m. and told them that they should be able to nab the girl, and the boy as well. The men looked pleased and excited.

As soon as Vanav got home, he went into his room which, considering that it was also their storeroom, housed the backup gas cylinder. Vanav waited until the coast was clear, when his mother was busy with her evening *puja* and his father had gone for a shower after his day at work, before hauling out the heavy cylinder. He secured it to the back of his cycle using an incredible amount of dexterity and intelligence to do so. Before setting off, he dipped a long strip of cloth into the fuel tank of his father's scooter and put it into his pocket.

Vanav was huffing and puffing by the time he managed to place the cylinder in an unobtrusive corner in the dilapidated building. Vanav unscrewed the top of the cylinder, looped the strip of cloth to the nozzle and hung the other end out through a small broken pane in a window overlooking the overgrown yard.

He was a little late getting back home from his tuition and told his folks that he had gone to a friend's house to collect some notes. He had his dinner quietly and then disappeared into his room. At around 9.30 p.m., he sneaked out of the house, with a little petrol in a used plastic bottle from his father's scooter and went straight to the godown and hid by the window where the petrol-soaked cloth was hanging. He dipped the cloth in fresh petrol again. Fifteen minutes later, when he heard the men come in, he lit the cloth with a matchstick and noiselessly moved away. By the time he heard the blast, he was far away. Before sleeping that night, he went over to Aarisha.

'This is for you,' he said taking out a bottle of Coke. For a moment, she was confused; and then she understood.

'Are you serious?'

'Old Monk mixed with Coke,' Vanav announced. When she unscrewed the bottle cap and took a sip, the life-affirming smile that lit up her face was worth all the treasures of the world and he felt he could walk barefooted over hot coals just for a glimpse of it.

Breakfasting beside his father, Vanav was glad that he had pulled off this escapade so smoothly. He polished off his breakfast and rode to school.

It was after he came back from his tuition in the evening that he found Aarisha alone on the terrace. When he inched closer, he realized she was crying.

'What happened, Ranisa?'

Taken aback by his quiet presence beside her, Aarisha quickly wiped her eyes and smiled at him, 'Done with tuition?'

Vanav nodded.

'Good.' She turned to go back downstairs when she heard Vanav ask, 'Are you homesick?'

She said, 'I'm hoping everything falls into place soon.'

'What does Daksh bhaiya say?'

'He'll come back tonight, and I'll know then. He said he has had a talk with his father.'

'I think you should talk to your parents.'

Aarisha sensed something in his tone.

'Why?' she asked.

'I saw some men asking questions with your photograph in their hands.'

'What? When? Where?'

'Yesterday. Don't worry, they won't find you right away, but eventually they will.'

'How did they find out that I'm in Ajmer?'

'On your first day here, you told papa that Daksh bhaiya smuggled you to Ajmer with the help of his friends. I think those men reached his friends first and then came here. But that's just my guess.'

'Hmm. D'you think I should call papaji?

Vanav nodded and said, 'Yes. But call him from a Public Call Booth (PCO).'

Aarisha thought for a moment. 'Coming with me?'

Within the next ten minutes, Vanav and Aarisha stood at a PCO booth. She called her home in Phagwara, Punjab. Her father answered the landline. The moment she heard his voice, she was swamped by the remorse and homesickness that welled up inside her; she released a loud sob and hung up, unable to say a word.

Vanav noticed her distress and was about to speak up when Aarisha put a finger on his lips shushing him. Adjacent to the PCO booth was a cigarette shop. Aarisha bought one cigarette and lit up. Vanav noticed that her hands were shaking badly. She didn't look at him, intently focused on her cigarette. As soon as she was done, she flicked the butt on the street and went into the booth again. Vanav stubbed out the butt with his heel. He saw Aarisha take a deep breath and dial again. After few seconds she said, 'Papaji?'

'Mona?' The moment her father spoke her nickname, she broke down again. Vanav stood frozen, not sure what to do.

'How are you, Mona? Where are you? We've been looking high and low for you,' her father's voice was marked with concern and worry.

'I'm all right, papaji. I'm in Ajmer. The boy I love is with me.'

'Beta, it's okay. Just come back home. We'll get you married to whomever you want. Just come home soon.'

'*Ji,* papaji. Please don't send anyone to look for me. I'm all right. Please give me a few more days. And . . . and . . .' she choked.

'Yes, Mona, I'm listening. Tell me . . .'

'I'll be back soon.' *I'm sorry,* she wanted to say. She replaced the receiver on the cradle and stepped out of the booth. Vanav mutely followed her. When they reached the house, they realized Daksh had already arrived. He took Aarisha upstairs and Vanav returned to his room. Vanav went into the bathroom and stared at his reflection in the small mirror on the bathroom wall. The image of Aarisha crying flooded his mind. Her shaking hands, the quick drags on the cigarette, her deep sigh before she called the second time and the way her body shuddered when she hung up kept replaying in his head. Vanav slapped himself hard. He couldn't do a thing to stop her tears. He slapped himself again and again and again, until his face went numb and he felt that he had castigated himself enough.

Daksh took Aarisha directly to the terrace. Before he could say anything, Aarisha updated him about her conversation with Vanav and that her family was aware that she was in Ajmer. Furthermore, she had promised her father to return home within a week.

'He has consented to our marriage,' Aarisha assured him at the end of her narrative.

'It could be a ploy,' Daksh seemed thoughtful.

'Papaji wouldn't plot against me. I know him.'

'All right. By the way, I too had a talk with Ma. She said she'll speak to my father soon and convince him.'

'But you said you'd talk to your father yourself!'

'Yes, I did. But first I think it's better if Ma breaks the news to him and then I take over.'

'If you think that's the way it will work out, then fine. I only care about this working out.'

'Of course, it'll work out, my love,' Daksh leaned in to kiss her. She pushed him away, saying, 'Not tonight. I'm not in the mood.'

'As if I care,' Daksh grabbed her hand, pulled her close and kissed her forcefully. Aarisha somehow managed to squirm out of his grasp, but not before biting his hand hard.

'Damn!' Daksh yelped. Aarisha laughed.

'I told you . . . not in the mood,' she reiterated.

'Yeah, but why bite so hard?' he nursed his injured hand.

'That is for when you return to Udaipur tonight. You can feel me in the pain that I inflicted on you.'

Standing by the terrace door, Vanav overheard the last bit. He was carrying two plates. Daksh had asked Mrs Thakur to send their dinner upstairs. Vanav went out into the terrace and handed them their plates. Later that night, after Daksh left for Udaipur, Vanav went upstairs to find Aarisha in her room, lying on the bed in a drunken stupor. The Coke bottle lay beside her on the floor. More than half of it was finished. Vanav walked over to Aarisha, took out the candle that he had stolen from the kitchen and lit it. He made Aarisha grip the candle in her inebriated state and held his arm above the flame. He gritted his teeth as the flame scorched through his skin. He held it there until he could take it no more and then extinguished the flame by tamping down on it with the burnt part of his arm. He carefully prised the candle out of Aarisha's fingers without waking her and walked out of the room.

As soon as he was in his room, he wanted to howl in agony. He touched the burnt area, tenderly at first and then viciously jabbed it. He bit into his pillow to mute his screams. The urge to shriek slowly subsided even though he continued to exacerbate the wound. Eventually, his facial expression changed.

If faces were books, his would read peace. Ranisa was correct, Vanav thought. The more pain he felt, the more he could feel her within him.

9

'Don't trouble her too much,' Mrs Thakur told Vanav.

Before he could say anything, Aarisha stoutly declared, 'He never troubles me.'

Pratap and Varsha had to attend a family function in Udaipur. At first, they thought they would take Vanav along, but Pratap suggested that it wouldn't be a good idea to leave Aarisha all alone in the house. As it was just a matter of a day, they asked Vanav to take a day off from school and stay at home with Aarisha. His parents left for Udaipur after an early breakfast.

Vanav was studying in his room when he heard her at his door.

'How do I look?'

She was in a Rajasthani *poshak* (outfit) with the complete set of jewellery to accessorize the outfit.

'Like a genuine Ranisa,' he stood up.

'I knew you'd say that,' Aarisha giggled.

'Where did you get that?'

'It's your mother's. I asked her for it, and she was kind enough to lend it to me. I wish to wear this for my wedding.'

'May I make a request, Ranisa?' Vanav asked earnestly.

She looked at him and then smiled, saying, 'I know, Thakur sahab. Give them to me.'

Vanav quickly brought the ghungroos out and handed them to Aarisha. She walked out, jingling them in her hand and Vanav followed her.

They were on the terrace. Vanav helped her fasten the ghungroos. She played a Rajasthani folk song on her phone. As she started dancing to it, Vanav sat down in a corner, utterly spellbound by the performance, staring, without even daring to breathe. Although his body was completely still, his mind was in a tumult. He continued to applaud long after she was done until she broke his reverie with, 'That's enough, Thakur sahab! Your special someone will get jealous if she gets to know you clapped so much for me!' She sat down to undo the ghungroos.

'Is it normal to get jealous seeing the one we love with someone else, Ranisa?' Vanav asked.

'Of course, it's normal. I remember once your Daksh bhaiya saw me talking to one of his friends. We had a terrible fight that day.'

'Just because he saw you talking to someone else? Why?'

'Well, he felt insecure. He felt that I could fall for another guy.'

Vanav thought for a moment and then asked, 'But even if you do fall for someone else, how will his love for you be affected?'

'As in?' Aarisha frowned.

'I mean Daksh bhaiya loves you. But is his love for you purely reciprocative; that is to say, only there until you fall for someone else? Can someone's love be so fragile that it depends on what the other person does?'

Aarisha thought for a while and then said, 'You're right. Love can't be so fragile that it pivots entirely on someone else's actions even if that someone else is the one you're in love with. But tell me something: hypothetically, if the girl you're in love with cheats on you and never tells you about it, then what will you do?'

'If she never tells me,' Vanav thought as he spoke, 'then I would never get to know. So, what I don't know, I don't have to react to. But if I do get to know, then I'll back off from the relationship, however, I won't abuse her. I'll respect her choice.'

'Won't you say anything to her?' Aarisha was a tad surprised.

'Don't you think, Ranisa, that when two people get into a relationship, it's because they want to add more happiness to each other's lives than there already is?'

'Yeah . . . I suppose so.'

'Then if the one with whom I'm in love does something that makes her happy, even if momentarily, and it comes at the cost of betraying me, I'll still accept it. I may get hurt and I may back off, but I'll accept it.'

Aarisha nodded incredulously and said, 'You're way too mature, Thakur sahab.'

'Is there something wrong with that, Ranisa?'

Aarisha shook her head, 'Nothing, except that it's the mature ones who get screwed by life the most.'

When Vanav offered to help in the kitchen as she fixed lunch for them, she was again pleasantly surprised.

'Oooh, you're so unlike your Daksh bhaiya. You don't believe that the kitchen is purely the woman's domain.'

'Gender roles have always confused me. Whenever I saw mummy making tea for papa even when she was running a 102° temperature, I couldn't understand why he couldn't make it himself. What was the problem if, occasionally, he did what mummy always does for him?'

Her smile full of irony, Aarisha said, 'I wish that people in general understood this; so many social issues would be eradicated then!'

It was late in the evening when Vanav came up to her room with a cup of tea. He found her listening to music.

'Oh my God! Don't impress me so much that I end up marrying you instead of your Daksh bhaiya,' Aarisha exclaimed, accepting the cup of tea gratefully.

Vanav felt shy and said, 'I've seen you having tea with mummy at this time, so I thought . . .'

'You *thought* . . . that's what makes you different from other men, Thakur sahab.'

He stood there admiring the delicate way she sipped her tea, squinting at the cityscape from her vantage point at the corner of the terrace.

'You know, Thakur sahab, it doesn't matter how much you love someone. There's always this dangerous pitfall. With time you learn to bury a lot of things which you would have otherwise shared with the person had you not been so invested in the togetherness.'

'I don't get it, Ranisa.'

'For example, I won't be able to tell Daksh that I want to continue dancing. I know he doesn't like it, but he does know that I love it. So, what do we do? One will have to yield to the other, otherwise the togetherness will suffer.'

'Why can't it be him in this case?'

Aarisha looked at him and a moment later laughed out loud.

'He is a *man*. And men don't cede to women. Or so the story goes, the one we have been fed since time immemorial,' she said, her voice dripping with sarcasm.

'Do you mean closeness destroys many things between couples, although it is closeness that couples seek all the time while they're in a relationship? Isn't that paradoxical?'

'It is. But then, so is love; so is life; and so are human beings.'

Aarisha finished her tea without another word. Vanav sensed that there was much more within her than she let on. Although she was deeply in love with Daksh, she could feel a certain discomfort as well.

The inherent contradiction distracted him from his single-minded focus on his studies that night. They had a quiet dinner after which both retired to their respective rooms.

The next morning, Pratap and Varsha returned from Udaipur. Aarisha opened the door for them.

'Aarisha, beta, I'm sorry but you'll have to pack your stuff,' Pratap said as he stepped into the house.

Taken aback, Aarisha looked at Mrs Thakur in mute appeal, but she averted her eyes.

Aarisha understood that there was some imminent bad news. Vanav didn't emerge from his room but eavesdropped on the conversation standing by the door of his room.

10

'What happened, uncle?' Aarisha asked, following Pratap into the dining room.

Pratap sat down at the dining table, looking thoughtful. Mrs Thakur sat down beside him while Aarisha, on tenterhooks, stood facing them both.

'Telephone your father. I want to talk to him,' Pratap said.

'But—' Aarisha started, when Mrs Thakur interrupted her.

'Beta, do as he says. Please.'

Aarisha dialled her father from her mobile phone and gave the phone to Pratap. She heard him assure her father that she, Aarisha, was safe and sound and with his family and that he would like to come to Phagwara personally to drop her off. He said he was taking the train that very night. As soon as the call ended, Pratap returned the phone to Aarisha.

'Can you please tell me what has happened, uncle?' she pleaded, her voice was brittle, and her eyes had welled up with tears.

Pratap looked at his wife, Varsha, prompting her to speak. Vanav held his breath as he continued to eavesdrop on the discussion at the dining table.

'Beta,' Varsha began, 'when we attended that family function, Vanav's father approached Daksh's father about the two of you because Daksh has dawdled long enough about this issue.'

'But . . . but Daksh told me that he has had a talk with his mother! And that she would talk to his father soon.'

'His mother didn't know a thing about you two. In fact, nobody there knew that you've been living with us all this while. That was when Vanav's father decided to talk to Daksh's father. And he did. It came as a shock to him. He confronted Daksh and . . .' Varsha fell silent.

'And . . .?' Aarisha asked. Tears were streaming down her face now.

Varsha braced herself before saying, '. . . and said that a girl who is brazen enough to elope with a boy couldn't become his daughter-in-law.'

'What did Daksh say?' Aarisha was finding it difficult to speak.

'He didn't say anything,' Pratap said.

A moment of silence later Aarisha marched up the stairs and dialled Daksh.

Vanav stepped out of his room. 'Can I go with you to Phagwara?' he asked.

Pratap nodded and asked Varsha to see to it that Aarisha got ready on time.

Upstairs, Aarisha tried calling Daksh several times but his phone was switched off. It infuriated her. Knowing fully well that the message may not be delivered, she still wrote one:

WHY DID YOU LIE TO ME DAKSH? WHY DID YOU HAVE TO BRING ME HERE IF YOU DIDN'T HAVE THE BALLS TO STAND UP TO YOUR FAMILY? OR IS IT THAT YOU WANTED TO SHOW ME YOU HAD THE BALLS, BUT YOU COULDN'T ACCEPT ME NOW THAT YOUR FAMILY HAS SPURNED ME? THE MOMENTS WE SPENT TOGETHER, THOSE KISSES WE SHARED, THE LOVE WE MADE; WAS EVERYTHING A LIE? I'LL HAVE TO LIVE A LIFE KNOWING THAT THE FIRST MAN I EVER LOVED WAS A SPINELESS SWINE WHO SWITCHED OFF HIS PHONE KNOWING FULLY WELL THAT I'LL GET THE SHOCK OF MY LIFE UPON LEARNING THE TRUTH. WHAT DID I EVER DO TO YOU THAT YOU HAD TO DESTROY MY RELATIONSHIP WITH MY ENTIRE FAMILY? YOU HAVE BELITTLED ME SO MUCH IN THEIR EYES. I DON'T KNOW IF YOU'LL EVER SWITCH YOUR PHONE ON AGAIN, BUT IF YOU DO AND IF YOU EVER READ THIS, THEN JUST GET THIS STRAIGHT: NEVER SHOW ME YOUR FACE AGAIN!

Pratap, Aarisha and Vanav boarded the Ajmer-Amritsar Junction Express in the evening. Varsha had packed dinner for all of them, but both Aarisha and Vanav were in no mood to eat. He had never seen her this quiet. It seemed as if she didn't know how to talk any more. As the train started speeding along on the track, Aarisha went up to the upper berth to lie down. Pratap was on the side upper berth while Vanav was on the side lower. At around 3 a.m., sleep evading his eyes, he went to the toilet and when he came out, he opened the door of the bogie and stood there, the strong wind buffeting his face. A few minutes later, he felt a hand grasp his wrist. It was

Aarisha. He turned to look at her. Her eyes were swollen and bloodshot with weeping.

'How do I face my father, Thakur sahab? I don't care what others may think, but my father . . . I've been a bad daughter, haven't I?'

Seeing Aarisha cry, he felt like someone had immolated him. This was the first time that she had grabbed his hand, and it was because she wanted to cry—and she did. Aarisha leaned against his shoulder and sobbed inconsolably for a long time. Vanav stood still, until her tears had dried on his shirt. Aarisha left quietly.

Vanav glanced at his arm where she had gripped him tight. Her nails had dug into his skin leaving marks. He caressed the skin there and looked up at the stars twinkling in the night sky. The cosmos and the gods themselves seemed to be taunting him, saying, 'we made the love of your life cry and you couldn't do a damn thing about it—not a damn thing at all!'

11

Aarisha's cousins had come to the station to receive them. Within fifteen minutes, she was home. Her mother wept as she hugged her prodigal child. Aarisha exchanged only one glance with her father; no words were spoken. Aarisha was taken up to her room while Pratap and Vanav were served tea and a cold drink respectively along with a large plate of hot samosas. Pratap apologized to Aarisha's father on behalf of Daksh.

'Although I don't have a daughter, I do understand your predicament. You know the kids of this generation: they don't think twice before taking a huge step. But I've done my best to treat Aarisha as my own daughter.'

Her father warmly shook Pratap's hand, 'I'm thankful to you for showing so much grace.'

'It was my duty. And do pardon Daksh's parents. They were completely in the dark about this situation.'

'Just as we were,' said Mr Shergill.

Pratap and Vanav were served lunch. There was no sign of Aarisha. It was only when they were about to leave in the evening for Ajmer, that she came down to bid them farewell.

'Thank you so much for everything, uncle,' she said.

'I wish you a very happy life ahead,' he said and turning to Mr Shergill, added, 'she is a gem of a girl.'

Vanav kept looking at Aarisha hoping to catch her eye, but she blanked him out completely. He followed his father out into the car that dropped them off at the railway station.

In the days that followed, he didn't hear his parents speak about either Aarisha or Daksh. The latter, he heard, was in Udaipur but didn't call or talk to Pratap. Vanav moved back into his room but, as he slept in his bed that night, he realized that the room didn't feel like his anymore. He lay on the bed where she had lain just a few nights ago. In one corner of this very room, he had seen her for the first time, in a bridal dress! She had appeared and disappeared from his life, just like that. Deep within he knew her presence had wrought a profound change in him, which her absence would now finish. He had retained her nose stud and ghungroos. She hadn't asked to have them back. He retrieved the ghungroo from his study table drawer and lay down on the bed holding them against his face. Soon enough, he found himself sobbing bitterly, wondering whether he would ever see her again and, irrationally for him, whether the ghungroos had enough magnetic pull to draw her to them and, by default, to him. All Vanav wanted was for her to be where he could see her. He had secretly planned to visit Udaipur from time to time as soon as she was married to Daksh, only to see her. He was okay even if she didn't talk to him—just the sight of her would suffice.

Time passed by inexorably. Vanav focused on his studies with the same avidity as he had done earlier but, unlike before, his bonhomie had evaporated; he distanced himself from Binny as well, which confused her because she hadn't a clue about his state of mind.

On the seventeenth day after Aarisha had been left at Phagwara, a letter arrived from the Shergill family, addressed to Pratap. Varsha placed it on the dressing table in their bedroom. During dinner, Pratap asked Vanav, 'When are your exams starting?'

'Two months from now.'

'There's enough time, then. I think the three of us can go.'

'Go where?' he asked.

'Aarisha's father sent us her wedding card. Haven't you seen it? It's on the dressing table.'

Vanav immediately thrust back his chair and tore upstairs to his parents' bedroom. He found the card and quickly opened it to read the main contents that were in a large red font, amid other information:

Aarisha

weds

Shubh

For a moment, Vanav almost blacked out. He tottered out and quietly returned to the dining table.

'Mr Shergill invited me as well,' said Vanav. 'Apparently, Aarisha told them how happy she was here, so they're looking forward to seeing us all there. I think we should go. They'll feel good.'

'I think so too. Aarisha is a such a darling girl. I don't know why Daksh had to be such an idiot.'

'Don't start that again,' said Pratap, 'I'm glad she's marrying another man and not an irresponsible buffoon like Daksh.'

Vanav's thoughts drowned out his parents' conversation. Aarisha was getting married to someone! He knew that this was bound to happen someday, but why did the news affect him so badly?

'Why aren't you eating?' Varsha asked.

'I'm not feeling very well,' Vanav said after a moment's pause. Abruptly abandoning his half-eaten dinner, he excused himself and went upstairs to his room.

Twenty days later, Vanav found himself at Aarisha's wedding. They were welcomed by her father himself. When they went in to see Aarisha, she seemed very happy to see them all. As the elders started talking among themselves, Aarisha turned to Vanav.

'Thakur sahab, how have you been?'

'I'm good, Ranisa. How are you?'

'Getting married, finally. How is your special one? Proposed to her or not?'

'No, not yet,' he said. *I don't think I ever will.*

'I hope she says yes,' she said.

Vanav smiled thinking, *if only I were that lucky.*

The Thakur family was ushered outside along with the rest of the *ladkiwale* (the bride's side), to await the stately procession of the groom's family and friends. Vanav remained behind alone, watching the pomp and splendour as the groom and his family marched in. After much ado, both Aarisha and Shubh were made to sit on decorated chairs on a small stage as it was time for them to exchange the ceremonial garlands.

Vanav found himself a quiet place in one of the common restrooms and crouched. He could hear loud crackers and gun shots, and people making merry, but he knew that he couldn't bear to witness the ceremony anymore. Hours later, his trance was broken by someone pushing open the door. He was surprised to see Aarisha.

'Ranisa,' he immediately stood up.

'Thakur sahab, what on earth are you doing here?'

'Nothing. I just . . .'

'I have to use the loo.'

'Oh, sorry. I'll leave.'

As Vanav was about to step out, she stopped him. He turned around. She leaned over, her fragrance filling his senses, and whispered, 'I know, Thakur sahab. I've always known. I always will. But know this, Thakur sahab, within this knowing of yours and mine, our story must live and die.'

Vanav, looked down at the floor, fighting back tears as each of her words resonated like a death knell in his heart.

'I had to agree to this marriage now that my whole family has seen how appalling my choice of a husband was. Shubh is their choice, my father's choice. As I agreed to the wedding, he is also my choice from now on. Shubh may not love me, not yet at least, but he has rights over me. Love doesn't bestow any rights, Thakur sahab, but a relationship does; and a socially accepted relationship even more so. By choosing Daksh I fell so far down in everyone's esteem, especially my father's, that I can't afford to refuse his choice. I'm sure that I too will eventually fall in love with Shubh over time . . . at least, I'll try to. And if not, I'll pretend, for marriage is a duty-bound exercise—and a woman is a slave to duty. Especially a married woman. You're too young right now, Thakur sahab, to understand much of what I'm saying. But one day you'll understand and then you'll understand why sometimes loving someone with all your heart and soul is simply not enough to be with that person forever. It's sad. It's depressing. It's soul-searing. But it's the truth. I'm sure you'll get over me.'

Vanav raised a woe-begone, tear-stained face, 'Won't we ever meet again, Ranisa?'

'We didn't know we would meet to begin with. It was destined. So, let the possibility of our meeting again be decided by destiny itself.'

'Aarisha! Aarisha!' she heard her friends calling out to her. 'Be quick! Everyone is waiting!'

Vanav turned away slowly and left.

12

Aarisha and Shubh lived in Delhi for six months after which they shifted to Rockville, Maryland, US. In those six months, there was only one way Vanav could reach her: Yahoo Messenger. He kept checking his notification every other hour to see if she had accepted his invite. After two nights, he was thrilled to see that his friend request had been accepted. He expected a message from her. But none came. There were no 'likes' on any of his pictures or statuses.

Aarisha kept changing her display picture on the trot. The more Vanav saw them the more he understood that they must be her honeymoon pictures. He started magnifying the pictures to a size where only her smile filled the frame. Vanav wondered why he couldn't have been the reason for her dazzling smile. He wondered how it might have been if he had been in Shubh's shoes—would she have smiled more? Or less? Moments are life's building blocks. And if you spend every moment with the one you love, life seems complete, fulfilling.

As the days passed, Aarisha uploaded more and more pictures of their travels to various destinations around the world. One aspect of the photos that stood out vividly was their obvious intimacy. Their proprietorial attitude towards each other made him uneasy; Vanav knew that she was his wife and they had the right to express their love anyway they pleased, but it still disturbed him deeply. It propelled him into a barrage of questions: who decides who gets whom? Is domesticated love the only form of love?

Vanav explored his own feelings for Aarisha. Even though he respected and loved her, he had no rights over her. Love didn't give one rights; a relationship did. *Ranisa was right*, Vanav concluded. The magnitude of one's love for someone is nothing compared to whether it is socially acceptable. If the relationship isn't endorsed by society, that love is deemed illegitimate. And illegitimate things are always swept under the carpet or kept under wraps despite the purity borne in its womb.

Vanav not only topped the XII standard board exams across India but also secured the coveted numero uno position in the All India Pre-Medical Exams. He also cracked a seat in the Armed Forces Medical College (AFMC) in Pune. The moment he got his results, he had wanted to share the joy with Aarisha, but that was not possible. The fact that she hadn't reached out to him yet was a sign for him to not reach out to her as well. And he had to respect it. For her was not 'her' man. He was, at best, the other man.

When the results were declared, Pratap took the family out for dinner and also invited Binny, who had secured a seat in the BSc course in Biology in Ajmer's Sophia College.

'When are you leaving?' Binny asked Vanav as he escorted her home after dinner.

'Next week.'

Binny noticed a subtle change in Vanav ever since Aarisha had come and gone. He had grown taciturn and had grown out of his silly shenanigans. They no longer colluded to pull pranks on others.

Although she long suspected that Vanav had harboured feelings for Aarisha, Binny never broached this directly for fear of having her hunch validated and she shrank from exhuming something that needed to remain buried. Binny herself had developed a crush on Vanav and if he admitted that he was still carrying a torch for Aarisha, that would only complicate matters. She was convinced that she would marry him someday; in fact, she had overheard her parents discuss this possibility; so, she wisely abstained from mentioning the elephant in the room.

'You'll be very busy this week, won't you?' Binny asked.

'Sort of, why?'

'I wanted to tell you something.'

'What?'

'You know I love you, right?' Binny exclaimed. She had rehearsed this moment several times but didn't expect it to happen quite this way—in a rush. Vanav went quiet.

'What's the matter? Has the cat got your tongue?' Binny demanded. As far as she was aware, Vanav wasn't involved with anybody; in fact, she knew that she was his only friend.

Vanav took a deep breath and said, 'You know people talk about "loss of innocence", but we rarely know the exact moment that we lose it.'

Binny looked into his eyes uncomprehendingly.

'I know when I lost mine.'

'When?'

'The moment I understood a very important fact of life: no matter how badly you want something, if you're not meant to have it, you'll never have it. And it's not you who decides what's yours and what's not. You can only decide who you want to belong to.'

Binny could anticipate what was coming next but prayed that the benevolent gods would strike her deaf before that.

'I've made my decision, Binny. I—'

'I don't want to hear her name,' Binny broke in hurriedly, 'and thanks for destroying my innocence as well! You're right, Vanav, we don't always get what we want. We can only con ourselves into believing that we've always wanted what we eventually get.'

'I'm sorry, Binny. I hope this doesn't destroy our friendship.'

'No way. It won't. If you can love someone knowing she's married, I think I can love you knowing you'll never be mine,' so saying, she turned away and fled into her house. For the first time, Vanav felt he had underestimated Binny's maturity. Or perhaps in the last one year, he hadn't realized that she had grown up too, just as he had.

When Vanav went home, he immediately pulled up his social media account on his computer. He went to Aarisha's profile. She had checked into a hotel in Peru. Her caption read:

Can't wait to see Machchu Pichchu.

Shubh and Aarisha travelled a lot, and Vanav stalked her display pictures relentlessly on social media—staring at each photo for hours. And then imagining himself with her at that very spot. That night he clicked on the message button and wrote:

HI RANISA, HOW ARE YOU? NOT A MOMENT GOES BY THAT I DON'T MISS YOU. I THOUGHT YOU WOULD MESSAGE ME AND I DON'T KNOW WHY YOU NEVER DO. DID YOU THINK THAT I WOULD EVENTUALLY FORGET YOU?

Vanav read and re-read the message and then deleted it. He wrote instead:

HI RANISA, HOW ARE YOU?

He sent it. The impatience of waiting for her reply gave him insomnia for several nights. Six days later, he received a reply:

HI, PLEASE DON'T MESSAGE ME. MY HUSBAND HAS MY PASSWORD. I WON'T BE ABLE TO EXPLAIN OUR RELATIONSHIP TO HIM. TAKE CARE.

Vanav read the message the night before he was scheduled to leave for AFMC, Pune. He stared at the message, unblinking, until he could no longer see it because his eyes had turned blurry. When he did blink, large tears rolled unchecked down his face. He noticed that he had been 'unfriended' as well. In her sky, he was surely that lone star that didn't have the right to twinkle.

What could she possibly tell anyone about me? Who am I to her? Nobody. So what if I love her more than anyone else in this world, where's my social license to claim it? Vanav cried his heart out the entire night.

13

Even though Vanav wanted to maintain a low profile in college, his brooding Byronic good looks and his knack of invariably topping each class earned him groupies. The fact that he paid them scant attention only made him more desirable. He was a challenge, unlike the rest of the easy-going guys in class, and therefore the most sought after. Some maidens wrangled for tête-à-têtes while others dropped broad hints that they wanted to be asked out. A few even made blatant sexual overtures. He ignored them all.

At times, alone in his hostel room, he wondered why he gave short shrift to his ardent fan following. After all, Aarisha was not his girlfriend. In fact, 'girlfriend' was much too heavy a term to use in this context—Aarisha was blissfully oblivious to the intensity of his feelings. If she had had the least inkling of even the half of it, she wouldn't have 'unfriended' him so callously. If she had wanted to stay in touch but considered social media too risky, she could have asked for his telephone number; but she hadn't done that. All she had said was that he was not to message her and to drive home her point, she had summarily 'unfriended' him. Her message was loud and clear: she didn't want to be in touch with him. When she had said that 'she knew', perhaps she meant that she knew he felt something for her but what was that 'something'? It could have been anything from an adolescent crush to true love and she probably assumed it was the former which would vanish the moment Vanav found someone else.

But he had experienced pain for her sake! *Can pain, in any form or extent, ever be anything but intense?* If she hadn't 'unfriended' him, he could have at least seen her updates, tracked her life and derived some sort of vicarious joy in her happiness. And still feel he was a part of her.

What if . . . she and I were in the US? What if . . . she and I had checked-in into that hotel? What if . . . that had been our honeymoon? What if . . . we were married? What if . . . she too loved me the way I love her?

Each time Vanav dwelt on it, he would hyperventilate and break out into hysterical laughter that eventually mutated into uncontrollable bouts of sobbing. It would invariably bring him to the same philosophical conclusion: loving another person with all one's heart and soul didn't suffice— there was no guarantee that the object of one's love would ever reciprocate one's love.

As days became weeks and weeks turned into months and eventually, years, Vanav remained trapped in the emotional loop. The nights were various, but the thoughts were the same.

One night, he had an epiphany: he should neither expect Aarisha to reciprocate his feelings and meet his expectations, nor should he expect her to stay in touch. She wasn't in love with him despite her kind words to him at her wedding. Anyway, as he had said to her long ago, just because a person isn't in love with one, doesn't—or shouldn't—alter one's love for that person. Is reciprocation essential to decide whether one's love will or will not sustain? The fact that he was in love with Aarisha was itself a happy phenomenon and he should be content with that.

These thoughts and debates that he had with himself had contributed to his maturity as a person; had allowed him to avoid the pitfalls and distractions of adolescence and youth; and had also, in more ways than he could tell, irrevocably altered his personality. He knew what his world constituted of: his studies and Aarisha. *So, what if I'm not anywhere in her world?*

Vanav topped the first year of his MBBS. A week before college was scheduled to break for summer, he attended a batchmate's, Neel's, sister's wedding in Mumbai along with his other classmates. At the wedding, he spotted a lady who seemed vaguely familiar. However, for the life of him, he couldn't place her. He kept an eye on her until it finally dawned on him: he had seen her on Aarisha's social media profile! She had commented on almost all her posts and pictures. If he was not mistaken, her name was Bijoya Ghosh.

'Excuse me,' Vanav said, approaching her at the buffet where she was selecting her main course.

Bijoya turned around. 'Yes?'

'I'm Vanav Thakur. I study medicine with Neel.'

Bijoya frowned, perplexed.

'Neel is Sushmita's di's younger brother.'

Bijoya took a few seconds to make the connection and then said, 'Oh, I see.' Not knowing what more to say, she refocussed on the buffet.

'Do you know Aarisha Shergill?' Vanav asked.

Bijoya paused and turned around. This time she looked at him with intent and interest.

'Of course, I know her. She's a close friend. Why do you ask?'

'I don't know how to beat around the bush. The thing is I love her. And no, it's not an infatuation or adolescent crush. I love her with all my heart and soul.'

'You do know she's married, right?' her voice was malicious.

'I know. I was there at her wedding. I had seen you there as well. But never mind that,' he shrugged. 'She actually asked me to stay away from her.'

'Then which part of "stay away" don't you understand?'

'I understood all of it which is why I never approached her afterwards. But I miss her a lot. And I saw you here and I wondered whether I could ask you for a favour.'

'I'm listening,' said Bijoya. She was all set to tear him apart as soon as he was done speaking. How dare he think of approaching a married woman? She had come across many such cavaliers in her life.

'I just wondered whether it's possible for you to let me know whenever she's in pain of any sort.'

Bijoya's expression changed. She had known psychos claiming to be crazy in love, but this one seemed to be in a league by himself.

'What? I don't get it,' she said.

'I know I can't be a part of her happiness or her enjoyable moments. That's because we celebrate our good times with people who are close to us. People who have a social license to be visible around you. I don't have that license. I don't think I ever will. Although I know my love for her is pure . . .' he choked at this juncture. The next second, he got a grip on his emotions, and continued, 'I can't feature in her life as I don't have a name for the connection I have with her. And when there's no name, people give it a label: illegitimate.'

'And what will you do even if I decide to let you know whenever she's in pain? You can't go to help her anyway.'

'I know. But if I were to know that she's in pain, I too can put myself in the same situation and share her pain. I don't want to be happy, even inadvertently, when she's suffering. I hope you don't think I'm mad. It's just that I feel happy knowing that she is well and cannot bear to think that I was happy when she was in agony.'

'I'll think about it,' said Bijoya. She had never heard of love driving someone to such bizarre lengths. Even though he had said that he wasn't mad and from his earnestness and demeanour, he came across as perfectly sane, she wondered, if only slightly, whether this was some form of mild lunacy or a certifiable psychosis which needed urgent medical attention or if it merely conveyed the intensity of this young man's feelings for her friend. She decided to give him the benefit of doubt but also decided to validate his credentials in some way.

'This is my number,' Vanav gave her a napkin on which he had scribbled his telephone number. 'May I also request you to keep this conversation a secret? If you tell her, she won't like it. Perhaps all this doesn't matter to you one jot, but if you have ever loved someone and died many deaths for them, only to want them even more, you'll know why this is so important to me. Lastly, be assured, I won't ever harm her in any way,' Vanav said before turning around and walking away.

Bijoya asked around and discovered that Vanav was a topper and brilliant in many ways. Therefore, convinced that he was not a nutcase but the genuine item, she only had two words to mutter to herself: 'lucky girl!'

It initiated a different kind of relationship between Aarisha and Vanav. This was a relationship in which one was aware and the other existed in total darkness. Bijoya messaged him twenty days later:

SHE TOLD ME TODAY THAT SHE'S IN PAIN BECAUSE OF HER PERIOD. DOES THAT WORK?

In the beginning, Bijoya wanted to share the incident with Aarisha. Then she decided to see how it played out. Plus, the boy couldn't possibly harm her from merely knowing when she was in pain.

Vanav replied:

YES, THANK YOU.

He was in his hostel room studying, when he received the message. He opened his medical kit and extracted a scalpel. He switched off his study table light and went out. Vanav arrived at the canteen a little before dinner. He asked the staff for some salt. As soon as he was given the salt cellar, he bore it off to a corner table. *If she was happy, he was happy. If she was in pain, he had to be in pain as well*, he thought and unflinchingly flayed his palm.

'I'll know I love her if I don't make any noise,' he murmured to himself. After that, he pressed the bleeding flesh on the salt mound. His jaw clenched. His eyes squeezed shut. And all the pain was borne without a sound.

Vanav started tracking Aarisha's menstrual cycle, confirmed it with Bijoya and repeated his skin-and-season process on a regular basis. On some level, it provided him with a sop. It wasn't that he had to prove to himself how much he loved her, but it made him feel as if he was sharing something intimate with her, something that even her husband wouldn't be sharing. At college, he watched his batch mates fall in and out of love. On the one hand, they talked about 'moving on' and on the other, claimed to have felt true love. There would be passionate declarations and a semester later, the time would come for 'true love' to 'move on'. Vanav didn't understand any of it. He was yet to find a reason to look beyond Aarisha—or rather, to think beyond her. Every relationship happens because the people involved see a semblance of some possibilities which are worth experiencing and fighting for. Vanav concluded that, maybe, when these possibilities die or the sense of seeking them is over, a relationship is done with. But in his story with Aarisha there was never any possibility of anything. And perhaps that's why he would never be done with her.

A day before his second-year final exams, his phone rang. Exhausted from his intense studying, Vanav was half-asleep. He wanted to ignore the persistent ringing, certain that it was one of his batchmates asking for last-minute notes before the exam but, after a few rings, he reluctantly answered the call without even looking at the smartphone's screen when he answered.

'Hello,' he said groggily.

'Hello, Thakur sahab!' he heard a voice say. He was wide awake suddenly.

14

For a moment, Vanav couldn't tell if he was dreaming or awake.

'Ranisa?' he asked, bewildered. His voice over the phone was sharp and clear.

'How are you? I heard that you're a man now?' she said, giggling softly.

'Can you give me two minutes please?' Vanav asked.

'Sure, let me call you back,' she hung up.

Vanav carried the phone into his bathroom and splashed cold water on his face. This was it! The moment he had waited for all this time! He had prayed to hear her voice, see her once again; he had died a thousand deaths thinking about her . . . it had been 1470 days since he had last seen her. He had so much to share but didn't know where to start. Should he tell her how he missed her every day, every hour? That she wasn't just an infatuation? Unbeknownst to himself, he was weeping with joy.

The phone rang again, and the same number flashed on the screen. Vanav wiped his eyes and accepted the call as he strolled into the balcony.

'Thakur sahab, all good?'

'Yes, Ranisa, all good.' *Now I'm used to living in your absence.*
'How are you? How did you get my number?'

'Why? You can get to my friend, but I can't discover your number?'

She sounded tipsy.

'Is that Old Monk speaking?' Vanav taunted.

'Napa Valley wine. I'm a wine person now. You see it's important in life to change preferences.'

'I haven't changed mine yet, Ranisa,' he replied.

'I'm glad to know that. By the way, why that weird request to Bijoya?'

Because I love you, Ranisa, he thought and said aloud, 'Why? Did you think it was weird?'

'You're young. There's so much to experience and learn. Why are you still stuck in a rut?' she asked. They both knew what she was talking about. Neither of them was direct.

'Tell me something, Ranisa. Why does the world consider me stuck if I'm faithful to one person? Just because I don't remain in her everyday radar? Just because I can't see or hear whenever I want to? Can't that one person have a certain universe in her that I may take a lifetime to explore? Why can't I experience the world through her? Why can't my journey be one that tries to understand why *our* journey couldn't be?'

'You'll never stop being so damn mature, will you, Thakur sahab?'

'Are you asking me to let go of the one thing that defines me?'

'Defines you?' she chuckled.

'How's life there?' He steered the discussion.

A second later she said, 'Pretty good!'

Vanav knew the answer was in the pause and not in the words she chose to answer his question.

'How are uncle, aunty? And that friend of yours . . . Binny, right?' she asked.

'All are good. I'm in Pune. Studying MBBS at AFMC,' he replied.

'So happy and proud of you. I look forward to the time when I will see a handsome army doctor salute me,' she said laughing.

'I am waiting for that moment as well!' *Our meeting*, he thought.

The way Vanav said it, Aarisha knew that there was a lot more to decipher than was apparent on the surface of his cryptic sentence.

He knew she was gulping more wine in the silence that followed.

'Find yourself a girlfriend, Thakur sahab. I don't like to see you like this,' she said.

'I don't need a girlfriend. I'm in love with someone,' Vanav replied.

'What if that love is a dead end?'

'It has already led to a lot of places within me that I didn't know existed. How can it be a dead end?'

'It's not good to squander your life like this.'

Vanav took a deep breath and said, 'One can choose to not visit a temple. But can one choose to stay away from God?

I can choose to pretend to love someone else, but will I be able to sever myself from my true love?'

'Don't save this number. I'll call whenever I can.'

'I won't appear in your life, Ranisa. Not until you want me to.'

'Thanks for understanding, Thakur sahab. Goodnight!' She hung up abruptly.

'Goodnight, Ranisa,' Vanav replied, and looked up at the cold night sky. The constellations continued to mock him.

He realized that every love story had an emotional epicentre. His story's epicentre was waiting. And he would do just that: wait. Not in a hope to have her in his life. But to see how much he could push himself being in love with her. A kind of love which had no expectations and yet it remained.

A month after his exams, his parents telephoned to say that Binny was getting married and they, all three of them as a family, had been invited to her wedding. Vanav immediately telephoned Binny, conscience-stricken that he hadn't contacted her for quite some time.

'What the hell! You didn't even tell me!' he gritted angrily.

'I would've told you tomorrow. When are you coming?' Binny asked.

'When do you want me there?'

'Can you be here day after tomorrow?'

'I'll be there. Let's talk then.'

Vanav booked his train tickets immediately and reached Ajmer two days later as promised. He dropped off his luggage at his house and went around to Binny's. The sumptuous decorations indicated that it was going to be a grand wedding.

There were many more people than usual milling around in the house. Vanav could identify some of her relatives and cousins. They were delighted to see him. Binny came out running as soon as she was told that Vanav had arrived. She grabbed his hand, dragged him into her room, locked the door and said, 'You're the worst *kutta* I've ever seen. Why did you drop out of touch? I know you did it intentionally!'

She was right. But had they been in touch, he wouldn't have been able hide the fact that he had been suffering from a deep depression and was unwilling to seek medical help. Vanav learnt all about depression when he took an online test about it and scored just as highly as he did in his academics. He, however, never let it interfere with his studies. He studied even harder and scored high marks but the depression persisted because he wasn't able to answer one question, the question which underpinned his deep-seated depression— *why can't I create memories with Aarisha?*—even if he knew that there was nothing he could do about it.

'Nothing like that—' Vanav started talking but was cut short.

'When did I become a problem for you, Vanav?' Binny asked.

'You were never a problem, Binny. It's me. I'm the problem. Even after finding an invaluable friend in you, I couldn't maintain the friendship.'

'D'you still love her?'

Vanav was quiet. She had her answer.

'Are you in touch with her?'

Vanav nodded.

'It's an obsession, Vanav. At some point in life, you simply must move on. And moving on doesn't mean you need to forget her. It just means you're okay with what life demands of you.'

It isn't an obsession just because I have chosen to be with her even without her permission. And if she were mine, then it would have been recognized as 'love'. Who decides these demarcations anyway? Vanav thought.

'Arranged marriage?' he asked trying to steer the conversation away from her.

Binny nodded.

'But I've told him straight up that I love you. And always will. If he wants to marry me, great. Otherwise, he can find someone else,' Binny quipped.

Vanav was quiet for some time and then said, 'I'm truly sorry, Binny.'

'D'you think I give a damn about your apology? Come on now. It's lunch time,' Binny said, and left the room. Vanav followed her out after a while.

When Binny wept bitterly holding on to Vanav during her *vidaai*, everyone thought that they were witnessing the most beautiful friendship ever. Only Binny and Vanav knew the real reason behind the tears.

Vanav returned to Pune the next day. In the days that followed, his depression took a maniacal form which manifested in anger. Every evening, he would punch his dorm room wall to vent his energy. He joined kickboxing only to channel his pent-up negative energy and would spend hours punching and kicking the punching bag. With time

Bijoya too didn't connect much, while he made sure he gave himself some pain on any one day in the month. In a way, he was happy Aarisha had unfriended him for that made sure he didn't see her pictures with Shubh anymore. But how could he unfriend his own imagination. He started masturdating: a concept of dating with one's own self. He went to movies alone. He went to cafés and pubs alone. But nothing helped. He could almost touch Aarisha's absence around him. Was it only love? Or was it love laced with obsession as Binny had told him? There were no concrete answers. While studying in his dorm room or doing practicals in the surgery room or attending lectures, he would abruptly burst into tears. There were nights when he went jogging and would scream his lungs out, taking Aarisha's name. He started enjoying saying no to girls who approached him for hooking up or for a possible date. He got a weird masochistic kick by turning girls away. He was living an irony. He told himself he belonged to only Aarisha but knew well she would never perhaps acknowledge his love for her. He had nobody to talk about his scars. As time went by, he was fast becoming akin to a house which had many people inside but no doors or windows. And it led to further depression. Until he met an unexpected relief, whose name was Samiha.

15

He first saw her at the Army hospital in Pune. He was helping a senior out with a case while making notes. Samiha was that senior's cousin. In the first week, they only saw each other; they never spoke. Then, one day, he heard his senior check her reports. Out of academic curiosity, Vanav too checked them out. He was baffled to find out that she was a drug addict who had been sober for the last six months. She suffered from acute agoraphobia which didn't allow her to go out of her house. She remained trapped within the four walls of the hospital. Much like him who was trapped within his own love for Aarisha.

'Why won't you talk to me?' she asked one day while Vanav had come into the room to take an update of her for his senior.

'What's there to talk?' he asked.

'How do I know what's there to talk if we never talk?'

'What do you want to talk about?'

'What puts you off?'

Vanav froze for a second. She knew nothing about him and yet she knew his deepest secret already.

'What do you mean?'

'I know that look, this subtle nervous energy. I've carried it with me for some time. I know you too are scared. I can feel it.'

Vanav was appalled by how this stranger had pinned him down so accurately.

'What's your scar?' he asked.

'My scar goes by the name of Captain Rashid Ali. If I have to name our relationship, then we were phone friends, but we loved each other. He was posted in Kashmir. After that, we had planned to meet in Delhi, but he was killed by a suicide bomber.'

Vanav noticed that her entire body was shuddering.

'What's your scar?' she asked, wiping her tears.

'Aarisha Shergill.' Vanav didn't know why he was opening up to a total stranger. 'She is married and in the US. I was never in a relationship with her, but I love her.'

'Does she love you too?'

'I don't know. Mostly not. But is that a reason for me not to love her?'

'Not at all. You guys in touch?'

'Not really.'

'Have you tried to be with other girls to move on from her?'

'I don't want to move on,' he said looking at her and then excusing himself. For the first time Vanav didn't cry. He realized in the statement he told Samiha that there was a decision. Why should he cry if he didn't regret the decision?

Samiha and Vanav started talking every day. There was a homely vibe to Samiha even though Vanav knew she wasn't her home. She would talk about Rashid to him, he would talk about Aarisha to her. They were like two storytellers. And then one day Samiha said something which changed their dynamic.

'Don't you feel like making love to Aarisha, captain?'

Vanav didn't speak.

'Have you masturbated thinking of her?' she asked.

Vanav gave her a sharp look.

'I have touched myself thinking of Rashid.'

Vanav averted his eyes.

'Close the door, captain.'

Suspecting what was coming, he did as he was asked.

'Come here,' she said. Vanav went and sat beside her on the bed.

'You be my Rashid, and I'll be your Aarisha.'

They closed their eyes and kissed. She had Rashid in her mind. He had Aarisha in his. What followed in the next hour was an emotional epiphany of sorts. Neither opened their eyes till they were done, exhausted in each other's arms. They transcended their physical being and connected to the soulmate they belonged to respectively. Their bodies were only a means. And pleasure was only a tool. Desire was only a bridge. As they climaxed, they moaned and grunted out names which weren't the others'.

Vanav dressed and was about to leave when he heard her say, 'Thank you, captain. Only two broken people know how to heal each other.' With that Vanav knew it wasn't a one-off thing. It became a trend and the more Vanav made love to Samiha's body assuming it to be Aarisha's, the more he felt he was discovering love in a way he never thought was possible. There was a momentary semblance of Aarisha's presence when he'd make love to Samiha's body, and that was enough for him to believe she was with him.

During his final year in medicine, Vanav was selected for a fortnight-long student exchange programme. He was scheduled to go to Johns Hopkins Hospital in Baltimore, Maryland—an hour's drive from where Aarisha lived with Shubh.

16

Vanav stayed in one of the hostel rooms at the Johns Hopkins campus. Just before he boarded his flight to the US, he contacted Bijoya and asked her to find out from Aarisha whether they could meet in America. When he landed at JFK airport, New York, he received a message from Bijoya saying that Aarisha would call him.

Although he constantly checked his phone for a message, a call or a missed call for the next nine days, it was only on the tenth day that he received a call from the number that Aarisha had used once before to contact him. As she had expressly requested, he had not saved it, but she hadn't forbidden him from memorizing it.

'Thakur sahab, someone is close now,' Aarisha whispered huskily, in her usual wine-soaked voice.

'Someone is always close, Ranisa. One needs to look within.'

'I know the medical thing is an excuse. You have come to meet me,' she had a naughty tinge in her voice.

'At least someone understood it.'

'Someone has understood a lot, Thakur sahab. She doesn't say it, that's all.'

'What has she understood? I want to know.'

'I know I've been a torture for you. But what if I tell you that from the last time we met, on my wedding night, we have stayed within the other. Does that make sense?'

Vanav felt his heart thud. He felt like a devotee whose prayers and emotional abstinence had finally been acknowledged by the Goddess.

'The essence of companionship isn't togetherness is what I've understood, Ranisa. Love is a soul choice, not a physical obligation. And when something stems from a spiritual decision, being present or absent doesn't matter. You are the person. And the other person is you. That's the power of a soul-connect. It doesn't let you be yourself only,' Vanav said and heard her sigh.

'You know, Thakur sahib, there are certain things which, till the time they remain within us, are called desires but the moment we talk about them the world assumes them to be regrets. My silence, my absence and my willing decision of keeping you out of my radar is that I can't let the world think you are my regret.'

'Even if you had made me your regret for the world, Ranisa, I would have lived it proudly.'

'You understand why "we" never happened, right? Firstly, I could never have said no to my father after how I let him down and then I feared with you around, I'd never be able to forget Daksh and what he did.'

'I get it. I'm not asking you anything, Ranisa. Except I'll be grateful if we can be in touch. I'm ready to live in the shadows, in the dark, away from your world but I just want to stay in touch. It just makes me feel alive to know you are a part of my reality. I've craved to hear you, to meet you, to . . .' Vanav couldn't speak any further without choking up.

'Don't cry, Thakur sahab. It'll spoil the colour of our love story even though there's not much colour in it,' she said, her voice choked.

'May I tell you something? I lo—'

'Hold on, Thakur sahab. Not on the phone. Meet me, look into my eyes, hold my hands and then say it. I'll know then that my belief, at least in one man, was correct.'

'I will. When will you meet me?'

'I'm traveling with Shubh right now. We are driving the whole day. We've just stopped at the gas station. He went to the washroom, so I thought of connecting with you.'

'Sure, I'll wait. How is Shubh?'

'He is good.'

'How is the married life going? Happy?'

'It's going very well. He is a nice man. My father's choice. Gives me whatever I want. Takes care of me. Respects me. What else does a woman need?' With the last part, she broke down.

'What should I believe in, Ranisa? Your story or your tears?'

'Just because something hasn't decayed, it doesn't mean it's alive,' she said. There was a prolonged silence.

'Come home day after. Shubh would love to meet you. Let's catch up over dinner. I know you like my cooking.'

'I'll be there.'

'Shubh is coming. I need to hang up. Hurry up. Don't keep me waiting, Thakur sahab. Come to me soon.'

Before Vanav could say anything, the line went dead. But this time he had recorded their talk.

The next day dragged out so incredibly slowly that it felt like time was standing still to Vanav. He couldn't focus on anything. Then came the day. The evening. He hadn't heard from her except for in the morning when she'd messaged him the address. He bought a bottle of Napa Valley wine and donned his best suit. The last time she had seen him, he was a boy. Now he was a young man. At long last, the moment that he had been waiting for, for years now, arrived. He picked up the bottle of wine and was waiting for his cab when he received a call from an unknown number.

'Hello.'

'Hi, this is Jude. Is that Mr Vanav Thakur?' It was an American man's voice.

'Yes, speaking.'

The man's next words were a bolt from the blue and the bottle slipped from Vanav's nerveless fingers and shattered on the floor, the spilt wine spreading over the beige carpet like plasma. Vanav hurried downstairs and told the cab driver to drive as fast as he could to the address that Jude had provided. Despite the cabbie's best efforts, it took him an hour to get there. Vanav rushed upstairs to find Jude waiting for him. He ushered Vanav into a dimlylit room. Vanav thought his heart would explode seeing his Ranisa covered with a white sheet which had bloody spots at several places. *Spot dead*, Jude had remarked seeing Vanav. He was the police officer who'd reached the accident site first. A trail of ten cars had bumped into each other owing to a truck's sudden stop on the highway.

One of the cars had Aarisha and Shubh in it. Shubh's phone was destroyed. Aarisha's was left. Jude called the last dialled number on her phone which happened to be Vanav.

With weak knees Vanav approached Aarisha's body. She looked at peace. The injury marks and dried blood had made her face ugly. Vanav had seen a lot of bodies during his practicals but never before had he seen one who he'd been in love with. He bent and spoke softly in her ears, fully aware that she couldn't hear his quavering voice. He gulped miserably, tasting the salt of his tears. He held her hands, but her eyes were closed as he whispered in her deaf ears, '*I love you, Ranisa.*'

Those were the words he had repeated in his mind, a thousand times, every single day, for years now, but had never had the courage to say them out loud. He had always wanted to but he had been waiting forever for the right time. And today, he finally did it. He finally said them to her, but it no longer mattered.

Aarisha Shergill was dead.

Vanav left. He couldn't feel anything. He walked on for a minute, then saw a speeding car crossing the street and threw himself in front of it. The car flung him in the air and threw him thirty metres ahead. He landed on his side and was unconscious immediately.

BOOK III
THE PRESENT

1

The news was broken to Aarisha by Pragya's father. When Pragya failed to respond to her messages or calls, even after several hours had passed since her last message, Aarisha feared that something was badly amiss. She waited until that night and then called Pragya's father.

'I received a call from the Delhi police. They have found a charred body which they think could be Pragya,' he said in a brittle voice.

Aarisha's throat went dry. 'How do they know it's her?' she asked.

'They found her Aadhar card in her bag and her telephone as well. They got my number from that. I'm already on my way to Delhi.'

'Was she alone?' Aarisha wasn't sure whether she should ask this, but her bestie was found dead, there was no time to hide anything from anyone.

'I haven't been told anything except that the Delhi police is waiting for me. I didn't even know that she was in Delhi. She had left the house as she normally did each morning. We had our doubts by the afternoon, but when we called, she said she was with a friend. That was the last time I spoke to her.'

'Uncle, I'm sorry but I knew Pragya was travelling to Delhi today. She called me from the bus that she had taken.'

'You knew about it?' Aarisha knew she deserved the accusation in his voice. She was an accomplice in some ways.

'She told me that she was eloping to Delhi to live with her boyfriend, Nimish, because she feared that you would marry her off to an alliance of your choosing.'

'She had a boyfriend?'

Aarisha remained quiet.

'What did you say his name was?'

'Nimish.'

'The police have already confirmed that the other charred body which has been found belongs to a guy called Nimish.'

Even Nimish is dead? Aarisha didn't know what else to say.

Pragya's father told her, in a defeated tone, that he would keep Aarisha updated and hung up. Aarisha tossed and turned all night long wondering if it was an accident. Why would they commit suicide? They were so much in love with each other. And if there was indeed a problem Pragya would have definitely told her. But that wasn't the only thing that kept her awake, it was also Pragya's second last message to her:

DO YOU KNOW WHERE YOUR BOYFRIEND IS?

This message and her death could be two unrelated events, Aarisha wondered, since the message came hours before she was found dead, but she couldn't help but wonder— *why would Pragya enquire about Vanav?* She did message him that night, but it wasn't delivered. Memories of the time she had spent with Pragya flooded Aarisha's thoughts. She found it hard to believe that her best friend was no more. Aarisha rushed into the bathroom twice at night and threw up before finally tottering back to bed. She eventually fell asleep exhausted.

In the morning, she telephoned Pragya's father again and learnt that the police had declared it was a mugging gone horribly wrong. Aarisha couldn't believe her friend's bad luck. Just when she was her happiest, death snatched her away, along with the love of her life; and for no fault of theirs.

She dialled Vanav.

'Pragya and her boyfriend are dead,' were her first words.

'How? Who told you?'

'Her burnt body along with Nimish's was found yesterday somewhere in Delhi.'

'What was she doing in Delhi suddenly?' Vanav asked. His voice, as always, cool and contained.

Aarisha told him why Pragya had gone there and then she told him about the cryptic message she had received from Pragya hours before she had died. 'I don't understand why she would send me a message asking whether I knew of your whereabouts,' she said, unhappily.

'Perhaps she wanted to ask me about some medical matter?' Vanav tried to reason.

'Perhaps. I don't know. Her last message to me was that she was making out with Nimish and would call me later. Can you imagine the kind of beast the mugger is to have killed a couple when they were making love? I hope that whoever did this rots in hell.'

Vanav remained quiet. He wasn't happy to have committed the double murder. But if he hadn't, there was a good chance that his meticulously laid plan would have unravelled completely. Once exposed, Aarisha would have been snatched from him and he would have lost his only chance of being with her which he had built up for years now.

'I'm not feeling good. I miss you so much,' said Aarisha mournfully. 'Can you please come over this weekend? I know you have work but . . .'

'I will. Don't worry. Just focus on your studies and take your medicines on time.'

'I love you. Absolutely.'

'I love you too. Absolutely.'

'Death is scary,' he could sense her shudder, 'it just snatches people away unexpectedly.'

'Death is indeed scary. But a life, after learning that someone who means the world to you is dead, is scarier,' replied Vanav.

Aarisha assumed that he was talking about his parents, so she changed the morbid subject. They talked for another half an hour or so before hanging up and returning to their daily schedules.

The next day was a Saturday and Vanav arrived at Udaipur as promised. He checked into a hotel. Aarisha wanted to drop by but he asked her to meet him at a restaurant for lunch. Later in the evening, they sat by the Fatehsagar Lake. She held his hand and said, 'I miss Pragya.'

'I can understand. Did you have a word with her father?'

'I wanted to, but I didn't know what to say or ask. I feel guilty that I'd lied to him.'

'It's okay. You did it to safeguard a friend. Not to kill her,' Vanav consoled her.

They dawdled for a long time over their post-lunch coffee after which Vanav asked her to accompany him to the hotel. Aarisha wondered whether he would take the lead for the first time and they would make love. She only wanted to hold him close and tight and sleep peacefully. As soon as they reached the hotel, to her dismay, Vanav asked her to wait in the lobby. He went up to his room and returned a few minutes later with a gift-wrapped box.

'This is for you. I wanted to give it to you the moment we met, but then we would have had to carry it around all day.'

Aarisha was excited to see the gift. 'What is it?' she asked eagerly.

'Open it after I drop you back at the hostel.'

'Can't I stay here with you in the hotel?' Aarisha pleaded.

'Not now.'

Aarisha made a face but knew it was forever a non-negotiable deal. Vanav dropped her off at the hostel gate. Upon entering her room, the first thing she did was rip off the wrapping paper and open the box. It contained a beautiful, figure-hugging fishtail prom dress. She immediately zipped herself into it and clicked a selfie that she relayed to Vanav with a message:

THIS IS SO DAMN PERFECT! LOVE IT.

Soni emerged from the bathroom a few minutes later complaining about her upset stomach.

'I should have had the medicine two times instead of once,' she said and stopped dead in her tracks, her eyes rounding in awe to see Aarisha's super-sensational outfit.

'Did he give it to you after you guys made frenzied, febrile, animal love?' Soni asked.

Aarisha's smile vanished, 'We did nothing of the sort.'

'Oh ho, and I had so hoped to distract myself from my stomach ache by hearing some raunchy details like the stuff in your diary. Honestly, didn't you do anything?'

Aarisha shook her head 'no'.

'Are you sure the guy in your diary and this guy are one and the same?' Soni teased.

'What do you mean?' Aarisha bridled.

'Just kidding,' Soni laughed.

Aarisha's phone buzzed with a message from Vanav.

GLAD YOU LIKED IT. I KNEW RED WOULD SUIT YOU.

Aarisha didn't know how to react to the text, because the dress he had gifted her was a beautiful shade of olive-green.

2

Aarisha telephoned Vanav at the crack of dawn, before he was submerged in his work.

'Why would you say the dress was red when you gave me an olive-green dress?'

For a moment there Vanav was completely thrown by her question. Then it struck him. It was a slip from his end. And only he knew that he could ill-afford such slips, however minor.

'Did I? Let me check,' he said although he was fairly sure he had referred to it as a 'red' dress. He was colour blind to some colours, especially red and green, so he realized that he had made a mistake. However, a few seconds later he came back with, 'It was such a lame typo, dear. My bad.'

'Thought as much. Otherwise why would you gift me an olive-green dress and then call it red?' Aarisha asked, comforted that it was what she had thought as well: a typo.

'I'm sorry.'

'You don't have to be sorry. Funnily enough, I made the exact same mistake once.'

'When?'

'I once wrote in my diary that I was in a "red" polka dotted dress when it was actually "green".'

'It doesn't matter,' Vanav said nonchalantly.

They talked for a few minutes more before hanging up. Vanav wasn't in Lucknow, as he had indicated to Aarisha, but in Delhi. At Samiha's place, where Pragya and Nimish had seen him. As he disconnected, he turned around to see Samiha watching him intently.

'What?' he asked.

'Nothing,' said Samiha, 'just soaking in your presence, so I can capture a better likeness of you on canvas.'

'I have a feeling that things are about to go sideways soon,' Vanav said.

'I hate to see such defeatism in my captain!' Samiha sighed. The bed springs dipped ever so slightly as she sat down beside him. Vanav pulled on his t shirt. Samiha put her hand lightly on his shoulder, stilling his movements, 'I've noticed that you seem somewhat stressed out these days.'

'I've done things that I shouldn't have,' Vanav's voice thickened with remorse.

Although Samiha was curious about those 'things', she knew better than to probe. If it came from him voluntarily, she would listen, otherwise she would have to live with the limited information.

'I'm sure they . . .' she began, but a glance from Vanav made her stop.

'I loved her without demanding or claiming anything. In that process, without realizing it, I built a bastion around what she meant to me. It was a fortress because I didn't allow anyone or anything to invade it and my love for her was a shrine within that acropolis. Sacred. Unimpeachable.

Unapproachable. Constant. Permanent.' Vanav went to stand by the open window and gazed into the distance with narrowed eyes as if he was contemplating something.

'And then, suddenly, destiny ran a fucking bulldozer into my citadel and the stronghold that I once thought was impenetrable, lay in ruins around me. I somehow managed to rebuild it with the bricks and mortar from the debris. And now that I've salvaged and resurrected it, I question myself whether it had been the right thing to do. I feel that I should come clean with her and tell her everything honestly, but . . .' he choked at this juncture and struggled to get a grip on himself before continuing, 'I know I'll lose her if I confess . . . and I can't afford to lose her. I once did. Not the second time.'

Samiha went over and hugged him from behind, her slim, strong arms around his waist, the curve of her cheek resting on his back.

'She never told me, but she'd tattooed the word Ranisa on her nape. Why did I have to see that tattoo on her dead body? It was so much more than a mere tattoo. It was her way of rebelling with her reality and reminding me that she was mine and mine alone. But she wasn't mine by "becoming" mine. She was mine by "being" mine. She loved me as much as I loved her. Just because she couldn't proclaim it to the world, didn't mean it wasn't love.'

'I don't know the kind of wrongs you've done,' Samiha whispered, 'but what I do know is that the reason behind your actions could not possibly have been wrong.' Samiha tightened her embrace and thought, *just the way I know that I'll never tell you that without you I will die.*

Aarisha was getting ready for her class. She was blow-drying her hair in front of the large dressing table mirror. She usually did that in the bathroom, but the plug point in the bathroom was acting up, so she had decided to use the electrical socket in the bedroom. Soni came up from behind her and said, 'I never noticed that before.'

Aarisha turned off the dryer and looked quizzically at Soni's reflection in the mirror. She was referring to the tattoo an inch below her nape. It was a gently arched 'Ranisa' tattooed in graceful Hindi script.

'Oh, this! He calls me by this name. That's why,' Aarisha explained, remembering how much she had cribbed when the tattoo was being made. But when Vanav saw the tattoo and caressed it with a smile, it had been worth all the pain. She recalled the incident from her diary, not from her memory.

'I think I'll also get a tattoo, although I am not too sure of what to get,' said Soni, her head cocked to a side like a little bird.

'Think about something that defines you. And then go for it.'

'My thought precisely. By the way, I've booked my tickets to go home this weekend,' Soni said.

Aarisha had completely forgotten that a long weekend was coming up and realized to her dismay that she hadn't planned anything. She also realized that it had been quite some time since she had paid a visit to her parents.

She decided to surprise them this time. When the day arrived, she chatted to them on the phone all through her bus journey from Delhi to Tosh via Dharamshala telling them she was in her hostel in Udaipur. They told her that life was boring without her around. When she reached home that afternoon, Aarisha was all set to spring her surprise on her parents, but her face fell when she saw the huge lock on the door. Perhaps they had gone to the market or out for lunch, she thought, and called her father.

'Papa, where are you?' she asked.

'At home,' he said. Only this time Aarisha knew it was a lie.

3

'All okay?' Mr Shergill asked.

'I'm standing right outside our house,' said Aarisha, flummoxed.

'What?' Mr Shergill sounded startled. 'Why didn't you tell us that you were coming?'

'It was supposed to be a surprise. But where are you guys?'

'We're in your mother's hometown.'

'Where?'

'Kasol.'

This was the first that she had heard about Kasol being her mother's hometown. Or had she forgotten that fact as well after the infamous 'accident'?

'What do I do now?' she moaned. 'Where's Dude?'

'Dude's in the café. Just go down to the café and wait for us. We'll be there soon. I've just asked your mother to pack.'

'All right.'

Dejected, Aarisha wandered into the café. Ramprasad was delighted to see her and Dude, needless to say, was over the moon. As it wasn't the tourist season, the café was fairly empty. She sat on a chair and Dude spread-eagled on the floor beside her. She telephoned Vanav. There was a faint tinge of shock in his voice when he heard that she was in Tosh.

'Why suddenly?' he asked.

'Just wanted to give mummy and papa a surprise, but they blindsided me. They're in Kasol, at mummy's place.'

'Oh, all right.'

'Sometimes I feel so useless! I don't remember a thing about my mother's hometown.'

'Just give me a minute,' Vanav said. He called Mr Shergill.

'Why did you leave Tosh without informing me?' Vanav asked sternly.

'We're really sorry, sir. We thought Aarisha was in Udaipur and wouldn't return until . . .'

'I don't pay you to think; I pay you to follow orders. Now get to Tosh as quickly as possible—and never repeat this,' Vanav said.

'We're already at the bus stop. We'll be there by this evening for sure. But I didn't tell her about our place.'

'Okay. Call me if anything untoward happens. Does Ramprasad have the house key?'

'No. We kept it with us.'

'Hmm. Get back as fast as you can!'

The moment he cut the line, Aarisha called.

'I just checked the distance between Kasol and here,' she said brightly. 'As it turns out, it's just about an hour's drive away. I was wondering whether I should go to Kasol myself and return with mummy and papa. I have a long weekend off and I can probably use this trip to refresh my stupid memory about mummy's hometown.'

'I think it would be better if you waited there. You must be tired from all the travelling.'

'That I am. Tired and somewhat restless.'

'So, take a nap. Isn't there a camp cot in the inner office at the café?'

'Why can't you come over? Don't army doctors have long weekends?'

'You've just gone and ruined my surprise,' Vanav groaned. Aarisha understood that he was on his way.

'Yessss!' she punched the air. 'I love you!'

'Really?'

'Absolutely!' She screamed out with joy.

It was evening by the time her parents arrived. They bustled in to fetch her from the café and the three of them went home together with Dude. Her mother hurried into the kitchen, clucking and chiding as mothers always did, and set about fixing her favourite dishes. She updated her parents about her studies and about Pragya's macabre death. They told her about their plans to refurbish the café with a lick of fresh paint. She made them promise to take her to Kasol the next time she was on holiday.

After dinner, she took the keys from her father and went out with Dude to lock the main gate. It was a ritual she performed every night before they retired to bed. When she had finished locking up, she turned around to see Dude bounding over with some paper in his mouth. Dude had been trained to play fetch and bring her any weird stuff that he happened to find. She patted his large head and gently extracted the paper from between his clenched teeth. They were bus tickets. From Baddi to Tosh. The date on them was today's date. They *had* to be the tickets on which her parents had travelled back. She went inside and found her father in the kitchen, deep in conversation with her mother.

'Why would you have tickets from Baddi to Tosh when you guys were coming from Kasol?' she asked, proffering the offending items to her father.

Mr and Mrs Shergill were startled by both her sudden appearance in the kitchen and her query. Mr Shergill took the tickets from Aarisha and after a cursory glance at them, ripped them into tiny shreds and binned the scraps.

'We had asked your mother's cousin to buy us the tickets. He stupidly booked us from Baddi, which is where the bus starts, but we boarded only at Kasol.' That was the best that Mr Shergill could manage at the spur of the moment.

'Oh, okay. Come on, Dude,' she called her dog and went away to her room. Mr and Mrs Shergill heaved a sigh of relief.

Sitting in her room, Aarisha tracked the route from Baddi to Tosh on her phone's map app and saw that Kasol was indeed on the same bus route. She roundly cursed herself for doubting her parents. *Why would they lie to me anyway?* she thought. She dozed off early that night after confirming on chat with Vanav that he'd left Lucknow. Or so he told her.

Vanav arrived in Tosh the next evening, and took her down to the riverbank where, she noticed, he had pitched a tent and set up a spit for a barbecue. While Vanav stacked the wood for the campfire under the spit, she marinated, seasoned, garnished and skewered the chicken which they barbecued slowly over the spit. Delicious aromas drifted over the river. Later, they went inside the tent, where Vanav had set up a gate-legged trestle table and a couple of deckchairs. They enjoyed their incredibly romantic candlelit chicken dinner and washed it all down with a bottle of wine.

'It's nights like these that make me believe that life can be a fairy tale,' Aarisha sighed happily, delicately sipping her wine.

'Indeed,' Vanav watched her intently as he drank his wine.

'I'm feeling good after a long time. Pragya's death had made me feel . . . '

'I can understand,' Vanav said, sipping his wine.

'There's something that's bothering me, Vanav,' she said. She knew that what she was about to say could compromise their current euphoria, but it was important that she shared her thoughts with him.

'Tell me.' He looked straight at her.

'Every time you go to Udaipur, you stay in a hotel. Even when I wasn't allotted the hostel room, you booked a separate room for me.' She paused for a beat before rushing headlong into the crux of her issue, 'The last time we made love was when you took me out on a date on this very river. Been more than a year since then. After that I sent you nude pictures of me, tried naughty talks with you and even dropped other broad hints, but you never reciprocated any of my overtures. Is something wrong? Haven't you forgiven me for the Dharamshala incident yet? What is it?' She was glad to be able to come out into the open at last with her thoughts and air her doubts after keeping them bottled up for so long. The wine was certainly helping.

'It's something I don't want to talk about,' said Vanav unequivocally.

'Does that mean I'm right? That you haven't forgiven me?'

'There's nothing to forgive you for, Ranisa. You know, when there's one spot on an otherwise clean cloth, people tend to focus on the spot. But what about the clean area around it? We all have spots and taints, Ranisa. But very few of us—like very, very few of us—have someone who chooses to focus on the clean part.'

'Then what is it that stops you from taking the lead? It's not like we've never made love before. Whatever you do for me is as much to do with care and concern as it is with passion. But where's the expression of that passion? Why is it so sporadic? For example, I want you to make love to me tonight, in this tent, under the night sky, but I know that unless I make the first move, you won't. Tell me, am I wrong? Do you think it's pure lust that makes me keep harping on this aspect of our relationship?'

'You aren't wrong at all, Ranisa. Nor are your desires. But I don't think it will make sense to you even if I were to confess why I don't initiate our intimacies.'

'Try me.'

'Sometimes the thing that you crave is the very thing that doesn't let you be yourself.'

'As in?'

'When you have too much of someone, physically, the mystery which makes for the togetherness, gets solved and is no longer an enigma. It's better not to rush in love, and let it flow slowly and be allowed to evolve and grow,' Vanav tried his best to explain the inversely proportionate relationship between love and sex and how too much of one could diminish the other. He hoped his hypothesis would satisfy her and make her drop the subject. He, of course, couldn't give her the truth.

'I suppose as long as you love me, I'll be all right.'

'And I'll be all right as long as I love you!' He came around to her side of the table, cupped her bemused face and kissed her forehead reverently.

'Nature's call,' Vanav announced and went out.

Aarisha finished her wine and cogitated about his profound hypothesis. Suddenly, she noticed a glimmer of light from Vanav's phone lying by his plate on the table. Someone was calling him. She leaned a little forward and her heart skipped a beat when she saw the name on the screen:

PAPA CALLING

How could his dad call when he was dead? Aarisha's eyes were fixed on the screen. The phone was on silent mode, so the ring wasn't audible. It stopped flashing after a while. She could feel her heart palpitate violently. She swallowed a lump as Vanav raised the tent flap and came back in. She turned away pretending to be so lost in thought that she was aware of neither the phone nor the caller. Vanav picked up his phone and checked the identity of the person whose call he had missed before he glanced at Aarisha again. She looked like she had seen a ghost.

4

Vanav felt that there was a strong possibility that Aarisha may have looked at his phone when the call came in. He excused himself and again exited the tent, this time with his phone. He called nobody and pretended he was talking to someone he called 'papa'. Aarisha didn't have to strain to eavesdrop on his side of the conversation because of the relative quiet around them, and Vanav was guffawing and talking quite loudly. She was somewhat surprised to hear the candidness with which Vanav chatted on the phone. A minute or so later he was back inside the tent.

'This friend of mine is certifiably stone bonkers!' he said, wryly.

'What friend?'

'His name is Captain Dr Parmesh Mathur, but everyone in our group calls him "papa".'

'Why "papa"?'

'Because,' Vanav said, pretending to hide a smile, 'he was the first one from our group to become a dad, at the age of twenty-five.' Vanav himself was impressed with his amazing skill at fabricating stories at the drop of a hat.

Vanav leaned close to her and whispered, 'Come, let me drop you home.'

She cupped his face in her long slender fingers and kissed his lips lingeringly. Vanav closed his eyes and prayed for the moment to end soon.

'As much as I want to, it's okay if we don't make love. Your love is enough for me to survive this and everything else,' she said.

Vanav opened his eyes and tenderly kissed her forehead.

Soon it was time to leave. Together, they quickly took down the tent and rolled it into a neat bolster along with the guy ropes, tent pegs and tool-kit; they took care to extinguish the campfire, ensuring that no stray embers were left lying around; they tidied up their camp site putting all their garbage into a large bin bag which they loaded along with all their belongings into the Land Rover. Vanav then dropped off a very sleepy Aarisha at her home, before driving away.

Aarisha was fairly certain by now that Vanav was hiding something. There was that time when Pragya had asked her whether she knew exactly where Vanav was and her lame reply to her bestie was that she trusted him implicitly. And she did. But what he had said to her tonight didn't make any sense. One can't claim to love someone and then avoid physical intimacy. Why wasn't he keen to explore the sexual side of their relationship? From what she knew, read and heard about single men, sex was not something that they would or could refuse, especially if it were offered on a platter. Pragya had said the same—that guys generally approached girls with the intention of having sex but cloak it in the garb of love. Vanav was quite the contrary. Aarisha was sure that all the passionate lovemaking described in her diary was initiated by her—even though her narrative pegged him as the dominant partner. He seemed to be progressively growing even more passive, sexually. She wondered whether she should be bothered by this facet of their relationship because, as far as his care and concern for her went, she had no complaints at all.

Vanav stayed in Tosh for the remainder of the weekend, telling her he was at a friend's place nearby but always putting up by a tent alone near the Shergill house. He left for Lucknow when she boarded the bus to Udaipur.

But she didn't go to Udaipur. From New Delhi she hopped on a bus to Ajmer although she told Vanav that she was back in her hostel. As soon as she reached Ajmer, she headed straight for Vanav's house. She had saved his message with the address.

All through her journey, she prayed that her suspicions would prove to be baseless and that 'papa' was indeed the friend that Vanav claimed he was and not who she thought he was. Arriving at the house, her first shock was to see that the lights in the house were on. Vanav had clearly told her that nobody lived here. From outside the gate, she could hear the television booming inside, Amitabh Bachchan's voice was clearly discernible as the KBC soundtrack swelled in the background to a crescendo. Standing there, she realized that she didn't have any plan of action. She dithered by the gate, furtively peeping in and wondering whether she should or shouldn't go in.

'Are you here to see someone?' Aarisha heard a woman's voice behind her. She whipped around, startled, a guilty look on her face and nodded.

'Hi, yes, I was just wondering whether this was the right address,' Aarisha showed the lady her cell phone—she *had* to do something so the woman wouldn't think that she was a potential burglar casing the joint.

'Yes, this is it,' the woman replied.

'Great! Thanks!' Aarisha turned to leave but when the woman reached over, unlatched the gate of Vanav's house and stepped into the garden, Aarisha decided to make further enquiries.

'I'm sorry, but do you live here?' Aarisha asked.

'No. I don't.'

'Who does?'

The woman studied her for a moment, surveyed the overnight duffel bag and the jeans-and-tee-shirt-clad figure, and asked, 'Whom do you want exactly?'

'Is this Vanav Thakur's place?'

'It is. And who are you?'

'I want to meet his parents. My name is Aarisha Shergill.'

As soon as she uttered those words, the entire demeanour of the woman transformed. A deep frown appeared on her face as if she had heard something absurd.

'Aarisha Shergill from Phagwara?' the woman asked.

'No, I'm from Tosh, Himachal Pradesh.'

'And how do you know Vanav?' the woman asked.

'Are you his relative?' Aarisha countered.

'Kind of. My name is Sumita.'

'Okay.'

'You didn't tell me how you know Vanav.'

Aarisha didn't know whether it would be wise to spell out her relationship with Vanav to a complete stranger.

'He's a friend,' she said evasively.

Sumita could tell that the girl wasn't telling the truth.

'D'you want to come inside?' she asked, holding open the gate invitingly.

'Are his parents alive?' Aarisha asked.

'Of course, they are,' she laughed, 'and they're right inside. Is Vanav all right?'

'Yes, yes. I've come on a sightseeing visit to Ajmer. He asked me to drop by and check if they were all right.'

'So why don't you come inside and do that?'

'It's very late now. Perhaps tomorrow,' Aarisha walked away briskly. On her way back, she realized that it had been a huge mistake to visit Ajmer. It would have been better if she hadn't discovered that Vanav's parents were alive and well but at the same time, she was surprised that he could lie to her so easily. But why lie about such a thing? Why on earth would he claim they were dead?

Sumita stood at the gate, baffled, trying to get her head around what just happened. She immediately scrolled through the contact list on her cell phone and telephoned Vanav. He was a little surprised to see Binny's name flash on his phone.

5

'Binny? All well?' Vanav asked. He was talking to her after several months.

'Where are you?' she asked.

Something about her voice set off alarm bells in his head.

'I've been posted to Lucknow. Are you here?'

'No. I'm in Ajmer. Dad's not well so I came here to see him.'

'What happened?'

'He suffered a cardiac arrest last week. He's all right now, but a little weak.'

'If you like, I can refer him to one of the best doctors in the country. Just say the word.'

'Thanks. I know I can always rely on you. But I didn't call you about that.'

Although Binny knew that they were great friends, she was also aware of how long ago it had been. She was caught between telling Vanav what had just happened and letting it go.

'Then? What is it?'

'I just met a girl outside your house,' Binny blurted out before she could change her mind again.

'Girl?'

'She said her name was Aarisha Shergill.'

Vanav understood that Aarisha had not only seen his phone screen when his father had called but had also not believed his impromptu fairy tale about the friend nicknamed 'papa'. And she didn't go to Udaipur from Tosh.

'What did she say?'

'That you're a friend and had asked her to check if your parents were all right.'

'Did she meet them?'

'I don't think so. I invited her in because I was on my way in to meet uncle and aunty. She said she would come tomorrow.'

'Okay. Thanks for letting me know.'

'What's going on? Who's this girl?'

'A friend.'

'Really?' Binny snapped. 'A friend whose name is Aarisha Shergill?'

Vanav drew a long breath and said, 'Keep out of it, Binny.' This was the first time in his life that he had been rude to her in a threatening manner.

'If you say so. But I hope you aren't doing anything that's going to have bad repercussions.'

'I won't harm anyone.'

'You've never harmed anyone but yourself.'

'I know what I'm doing.'

'So, this is not what it seems like, huh? I wish you good luck.'

'I'm sorry but—' Binny had already hung up.

He knew he shouldn't have talked to her the way he did, but he had had no other option. He couldn't tell her what he had been up to for years now and why he had done it. He knew Binny wouldn't shove her oar in, but what about Aarisha now that she knew that his parents were alive? He weighed the pros and cons and then called her. The reception was poor, and they had trouble hearing each other.

Seconds later Aarisha texted him.

Aarisha: CAN WE TEXT PLEASE? NETWORK SUCKS HERE. I'M IN THE TRAIN.

Vanav: SURE, WHERE ARE YOU?

Aarisha: I WAS IN AJMER WITH SONI. NOW ON MY WAY BACK. MET HER AT DELHI AND SHE PULLED ME TO AJMER BECAUSE HER BOYFRIEND'S FAMILY HAD COME TO VISIT THE DARGAH.

Vanav: YOU DIDN'T TELL ME ABOUT IT. I THOUGHT YOU WERE IN UDAIPUR.

Aarisha: I WAS ON MY WAY BACK, BUT UNEXPECTEDLY GOT SIDE-TRACKED TO AJMER. I HAD TO ACCOMPANY SONI EVERYWHERE. I'M SORRY.

Vanav: IT'S OKAY.

Aarisha: LET ME CALL YOU THE MOMENT I REACH UDAIPUR.

Vanav: I'LL WAIT. TRAVEL SAFE.

There was no mention of her going to his house and learning about his parents being alive. Vanav realized that she was deliberately withholding that information. It could mean one of two things: one, she didn't really care that he was lying to her; two, the lie meant a little too much and his duplicity was setting off her alarm bells.

Aarisha was indeed in a train, but she wasn't going to Udaipur. She was returning to Delhi from where she would board the bus back to Tosh. After the shock of tonight's discovery, the realization that Vanav could lie to her so brazenly opened an emotional Pandora's box within her. She had started to think back about her entire life. She couldn't remember anything of her childhood, her college and not even the accident. Whatever she knew about her own life was primarily from her parents, her diary and bits and pieces gleaned from Vanav. There was nothing about herself that she could be conclusively sure of because her memory was as good as non-existent.

She reached her house and found it locked once again. She called her parents casually, talked about mundane things and then asked, 'Where are you both?'

'At home. Where else?'

'Tosh or Kasol?' she wanted to be specific this time.

'Kasol is mother's place. Tosh is our home.'

And with that Aarisha knew she was trapped in a strange conspiracy. She had only two worlds until then: her parents and Vanav. And now they both seemed to be colluding to conceal things from her.

Binny, while talking to Vanav's parents, was lost. There was something wrong both about the girl and Vanav. And her gut told her it wasn't possible that the girl's name being Aarisha Shergill was a coincidence.

'Don't you two ask Vanav to get married?'

'There was a time but now I think he has crossed that age when anyone would want to marry him,' Mrs Thakur said. There was deep-seeded grief in her voice. Binny understood Vanav had told them about no girl yet.

'Any news of Aarisha?' Binny blurted out. Both Mr and Mrs Thakur glanced at her as if they didn't remember the name. And then suddenly Mr Thakur said, 'So unfortune. She died in a car accident with her husband. They were so young. Been years now.'

'Who told you?'

'Vanav told us,' Mrs Thakur said.

'If I remember clearly, she was from Phagwara?'

'Yes. The Shergills of Phagwara. They had a name. Vanav and I had gone there twice . . . ' Mr Thakur started talking as if revelling in good old times while Binny's brain was working fast. She was supposed to visit her in-laws with her husband in a week to Jalandhar and Phagwara was twenty-five odd kilometres from there. She took her leave after a few minutes of banter.

Aarisha returned to Udaipur the next day. In the meanwhile, she avoided talking to Vanav on the telephone—dodging with one excuse after another. She was sure he wasn't going to tell her anything. And even if he did, how could she trust him now? Her perfect boyfriend was turning out to be a barefaced liar. She fought the impulse of confronting him and her parents directly about all this. But by now she knew that they would tell her to justify it all and that it may not be the truth. She had to find the truth herself. The only thing she didn't know was how.

The morning, Aarisha reached her institute, Soni told her that she was required to fill out a form. The MBA institute, in collaboration with a women's health NGO, had set up a free medical check-up for all its female students. One by one, every girl from the first-year batch underwent the check-up. When it was her turn, Aarisha entered the makeshift examination cubicle. Her full body check-up revealed no abnormalities. When the gynaecologist checked her genitals, inserting a vaginal camera as she had done with the other girls, for diagnosing possible PCOD (Polycystic Ovary Syndrome), she told Aarisha something that made her head spin. Aarisha was told she was only the second girl in the whole batch whose hymen was still intact. She was a virgin.

6

Aarisha found that statement so funny that she laughed uproariously; but when the mystified doctor didn't join in her mirth, Aarisha realized that the medic was dead serious.

'I've had a boyfriend for some time now,' Aarisha said, hoping that she wouldn't have to expand on this and spell it out to the gynaecologist.

'So?'

'I'm not a virgin.'

'It happens. If you've had sex one time, the hymen may not have broken. Nothing to worry about.'

And that was when her head started spinning faster.

We've had sex several times, she thought, but didn't say anything further to the doctor. She was told that the reports of all her tests would be emailed to her.

Aarisha went straight to her room and sat down with her diary. She was alone in the dorm room because Soni was downstairs, still awaiting her turn for the medical check-up. Aarisha started re-reading all her diary entries, especially the sections where details of her lovemaking with Vanav had been recorded. After what she had learnt of Vanav and her parents, she felt as if her diary was the only thing that she could trust as it had been written by her own self. But now even that was coming into question. All those moments that she had revelled in, relying not on her memory but on her imagination and the entries documented in her diary, about the perfect world that she had been a part of before her accident, were mere figments of her imagination? It didn't answer why Vanav never initiated anything sexual with her, but why would she write about moments that never happened? On that memorable date night, she was on a boat with Vanav on the Tosh river. She remembered that much. And he did tell her the next morning that they had made love. The proof of which was right there, in the diary, in black and white. Or was it that he never penetrated her? Was she really a virgin? She wanted to call Vanav instantly, but she knew that she could no longer trust his words. She knew that she would have to investigate these anomalies herself.

When Soni came into the room, Aarisha had one question ready for her: can someone's virginity return? Soni gave her a look, punched something on her phone and then hurled the phone towards her, and herself went inside the washroom. Aarisha took the phone and noticed the screen was showing Google results for her query. And one of the links in the results talked about certain hymen reconstruction surgeries. And Vanav was a surgeon. Aarisha's head was reeling. She kept the phone away.

Aarisha skipped her classes, her food and her studies and sat cooped up in the library for hours, thinking, re-thinking, analysing and re-analysing everything she knew or thought she knew. She minutely examined all the incongruities about her parents, Vanav and her diary. She concluded that her life had to be divided into two sections—pre-accident and post-accident. Pre-accident was probably normal. Post-accident wasn't. Her amnesia about the pre-accident phase had been triggered by the accident that her parents and Vanav had always referred to as a 'bad' incident. And now that she had lost faith in her parents as well as Vanav, she decided she needed to determine whether the 'bad' incident was indeed an accident.

She clearly remembered that her mother had told her that the accident had happened in Solan, near her college, while Pragya had mentioned that she had seen police at her place after the incident. It could only mean that the case had been registered with the local police.

When Vanav telephoned that night, she pretended that everything was just fine except for semester exam pressure. She didn't want him sniffing around until she understood the aberrations about her past.

Vanav called Samiha after he was done with the last surgery of the day in the command hospital in Lucknow. It took Samiha by surprise because they rarely talked on the phone.

'Captain, all good?' she asked.

'I don't think so.' He sounded lost which was unlike him.

'What happened?' She never asked him direct questions but this time she couldn't help herself. There was something he wanted to talk about.

'She knows my parents are alive but still hasn't told me about it.'

'How did she find out?' She was slightly shocked.

'Doesn't matter. The fact that she knows and didn't mention it to me tells me she knows I'm a liar.'

'Does she know why you lied?'

'At least now she is pretending. Do you think she will be with me if she knows the truth?'

'So, what do you have in mind?'

'What do you do when you know your most feared nightmare is about to come true?'

'You take some action to avoid it.'

'Not when the person who is going to make those nightmares true for you is the one you love.'

'What are you hinting at, captain?'

'I tried my best to live a dream with her. I did to an extent. But now if I must live the nightmare, I'll do that as well. For her.'

There was silence after which Vanav spoke, 'If she understands I'm a liar, if she gets to the truth, she isn't going to hate me, right?' His voice was choked.

'Captain, she will never be able to hate you if she understands the reason behind all this.'

After a moment's silence, Vanav ended the call, saying, 'I hope.'

The next week, without a scrap of compunction, Aarisha lied to her parents and Vanav that she had joined a group of girls on a trek to Triund, and then made her way to Solan. When Vanav did a bit of digging around, using his contacts in the railways to cross-check, Aarisha's story tallied: there *was* a group of girls who were to travel to New Delhi from Udaipur in the Mewar Express and one of them was Aarisha Shergill. He asked about the hotel into which Aarisha was booked into and then telephoned the hotel in Dharamshala to double check the number of girls checking-in and once again she was included in the number. However, while her friends had set off on their trek to Triund, Aarisha had hired a cab to Solan.

As soon as she arrived at Solan, Aarisha hurried to the police station and asked for the FIR details about an accident case in the name of Aarisha Shergill. She gave them the date of the accident indicated in her diary. However, although they looked high and low for it, they found no FIR in the name of Aarisha Shergill; furthermore, they could find nothing on their logs on the date that she provided although they helpfully increased the range and checked other dates within two months preceding and following the indicated date. When she told them she lived in Tosh, they suggested that perhaps the Kullu police station would be able to help her out.

Aarisha returned to the hotel in Dharamshala. A day later, she travelled to Kullu, this time with Soni. She introduced herself to the policeman at the desk and furnished him with the date of the accident. The corrupt police officer had to be bribed into doing a search. After half an hour of poring through the records, he told her that there was one FIR lodged in the name of Aarisha Shergill. The date was the same as mentioned in her diary. But it wasn't an accident case. It was a rape and molestation case.

Aarisha froze. Finally, the 'bad' incident made sense. She had been raped. Perhaps that was why she had shut out the memories of the incident and the inexplicable gaps in her memory had begun to appear. She had never felt so confused about her loved ones before. On the one hand, she had her parents and Vanav to thank for their stalwart support and tender care after such a heinous incident; and on the other, she no longer trusted them. Emerging from the police station, she broke down and wept in the cab and Soni consoled her.

'Calm down dear,' Soni patted her back. 'Let bygones be bygones. I know it's the worst shit possible but look on the brighter side: you have such a caring family and a loving boyfriend. In fact, your boyfriend cares for you so much that he has given you those medicines.'

Aarisha looked up at that and wiped her tears, 'What medicines?'

'The ones you take daily. I've got a BPharm degree. I know what those medicines are, but I always wondered why they were prescribed to you. Especially since you are on a high dose. I thought it was something personal, so I never asked you about it. Remember how you freaked out when you saw me reading your diary? I know that was wrong on my part, so I decided not to probe. But now all of it makes sense . . .'

Aarisha was lost in her own thoughts. Her face reflecting her growing anxiety.

'That was why I always said that you were very lucky to have such a wonderful boyfriend. He could have avoided the high dosage of propranolol, but he did it to help you forget and get over the bad thing that had happened. It's given to patients to treat PTSD (post-traumatic stress disorder).'

There was silence.

'Don't worry about it, I promise not to discuss this with anyone,' Soni said, guessing that that was what was bothering Aarisha.

So that you can forget about the bad thing, Soni's words echoed loud in her mind, or *did he do it to alter my memory?*

7

Binny, as per her plan with her husband and kid, reached Jalandhar. They were visiting the place after two years. Anurag's father died a few years back. While he had kept his mother with him in Delhi, his brothers still lived in the old family house in Jalandhar. Everyone was delighted to see them. Especially Sirat.

What was not in the plan was Binny's travel plan to Phagwara. She told Vinod, her younger brother-in-law, about it.

'I'll take you there, bhabhi. It's not that far.'

The next morning, Vinod took Binny to Phagwara. It was a mere half an hour's drive from Jalandhar. Once there, they asked around. During her recent visit to Vanav's place in Ajmer, Binny had asked Pratap if he had Aarisha's address. Though Varsha lamented that it was years back that Pratap had gone with Vanav to drop her, Pratap said he should have the address. He had the habit of preserving everything. He went into his room and came out ten minutes later with an invitation card in his hand. He gave it to Binny.

Sitting in the SUV with Vinod, Binny had Aarisha's wedding card in her hand. She was constantly asking around for the address written on it. Soon they were there. The house they'd parked outside looked lifeless. It was dismal. Binny asked Vinod to stay where he was, inside the car, while she went in. While Binny was opening the gate, an old lady sitting by the garden asked, 'Whom do you want?'

'Is this Aarisha Shergill's house?' Binny asked.

The lady stared at her for some time and then said, 'It is. Who are you?'

'I'm an old friend.'

The old lady ushered Binny into the house. Binny learnt that the lady was Aarisha's bhabhi. A minute later, Mrs Shergill entered the drawing room. She was wearing a white salwar kameez and looked frail.

'I never saw you with Mona ever.'

'Mona?' Binny asked.

'Mona was Aarisha's nick name,' Aarisha's bhabhi clarified.

'I'm sorry, aunty, I wasn't that close a friend of hers. And I'm also sorry to barge in on you like this but I wanted to know few things about her.'

'Things like?' Mrs Shergill asked.

'I know it may sound wrong, but may I know where Aarisha's husband is?' Binny asked. All Vanav had ever told her was Aarisha had died. He never told her about Shubh. Nor had she asked him before.

'They both died in a car accident,' the bhabhi replied.

'Oh! I'm sorry. Did they have any . . .' Binny didn't know how to put it.

'No, they never had any kids if that's what you want to ask. I remember it was a bad morning. Someone from the US had called us to inform us that Shubh and she died in a car accident. Her father could never recuperate from the news.'

'Who was the caller?' Binny asked the bhabhi.

'A man, I remember. I'd picked up the call that morning.'

'Someone from the family?'

'No. He said he was a friend of Aarisha's.'

Binny didn't know what else to ask. In fact, she didn't know why she was there in the first place. She didn't have a specific agenda in mind. Something about the girl who claimed to be Aarisha Shergill had disturbed her. But she'd told her she wasn't from Phagwara but Tosh. Had Phagwara not been so close to Jalandhar she wouldn't have allowed the curiosity to corner her. Binny took her leave after a few minutes. It was while going back to Jalandhar with Vinod that she called Vanav's mother.

'Aunty, has Vanav been to the US in the past?'

'Yes. Once he'd gone to the US when he was still studying medicine in Pune. Why, what happened?'

'Nothing. Can you tell me what month it was?'

The answer made Binny think. Vanav was there on the same month Aarisha had died. Could he be the person who called her home to relay the news? But even if he was, then what was the problem? There was something niggling her mind. But she didn't know what. Binny saved the phone number which Aarisha's bhabhi had given her. It was Shubh's home number. She was told he was from Delhi. After some time, Binny took her leave.

Aarisha and Soni had gone a mile from the Kullu police station when Aarisha suddenly asked the driver to take a U-turn for the police station once again.

'What happened? You forgot something there?' Soni asked.

Aarisha didn't answer. Soni understood that she should remain quiet.

Once they reached the police station, Aarisha went to the inspector on duty and asked, 'Didn't anyone come here ever to enquire who those men were?'

'Not that I can recall.'

Even after knowing I was raped, Vanav never contacted the police to know who did this? Not even once, Aarisha wondered.

'Thank you,' she said. As she was stepping out of the police station, she overheard a couple of constables talking. They were talking about the dead bodies of three boys who had come to Tosh for a vacation.

8

Aarisha took her phone and pretended to type something but she was alert and absorbing every word the constables were exchanging outside the police station.

'The party is rich. They are from Mumbai. If we tell them these bodies are their sons, then we can milk them for some money,' said one of the constables.

'But they will find out these three aren't those three, then?' said the second.

'When they find out that it's not their sons' bodies we can always tell them that we were relaying what our seniors had told us.'

'Sounds like a plan. Let's have some tea first and then gets this plan rolling.'

The constables traipsed off while Aarisha messaged Soni:

Coming in two minutes

She turned and went right into the police station.

'Has anyone registered a case of three boys going amiss about a year or so back?' she asked the inspector in charge.

He looked up at Aarisha, irritated. Why did this girl keep digging up old things?

'Three boys from some respected family had gone missing in Tosh. Since they belonged to a few powerful families our asses have been on fire from the higher authorities. But how does it matter to you?'

'May I please look at their photographs?'

'Why?'

'I've stayed here for long. Maybe I'll recognize them,' Aarisha said.

The inspector gave her a long look before getting up. As he went to a steel almirah to bring out a file, she prayed that her hunch was wrong. The inspector came back to his seat and opened the file, taking out three photographs. He handed them to Aarisha. She didn't have to look at all three. The first one was of the guy who had slapped her butt. She remembered him clearly. Her hands were shivering as she held the photograph. But not because she recognized the guy. It was the police report in front of her.

The first line of the report was about the call the police received at a certain time from an unknown person who claimed to be from the Army, but his phone number had been untraceable. It was the same first line in her rape report as well. A man had called, not an Army guy though, whose number had later been untraceable.

'Their bodies were never found?' Aarisha asked.

'Not yet. At least we got a phone call from this unknown person who saw them by the Tosh river. Our conclusion is that they must have gotten so drunk that they got into the river and then were washed away. It has happened many times here and elsewhere nearby. But do you recognize any of them?'

'No. I'm sorry,' Aarisha said and walked out of the police station with one thought: kill them. Then call the police anonymously stating he saw them by the river. Knowing well they won't be found. But still the police would think they may have washed away by the river. Could this be a plan? And could the man be . . .

Aarisha thought her heart would explode any moment.

'What happened?' Soni asked.

'I'm not in the right state of mind to talk,' Aarisha said and remained silent throughout her journey knowing well she could be right, but she couldn't stop the tears which were a sign of a conscious conclusion her mind was making about Vanav. And she didn't want to believe one bit of it.

All through Binny's journey from Jalandhar to Delhi, she kept wondering what exactly she was doing. Snooping around people's houses and behind her once best-friend and forever love's back, but then her gut told her that something was wrong with Vanav. Something which she could have sensed earlier had she been in touch with him more often. He had withdrawn even more after Aarisha's death. Before that at least he used to be traceable and somewhat within reach but in the last ten to twelve years she could count how many times they had talked on the phone forget about meeting each other. By the time she reached Delhi, she had convinced herself that she was right in doing so. For if Vanav was in any trouble, she could ward it off. But she knew Vanav himself wouldn't tell her about any of his problems. He never told her about this Aarisha Shergill of Tosh.

The first thing Binny did after reaching Delhi two days later was to call Shubh's home. She told them she wanted to talk about Shubh and his wife Aarisha and thus wanted to meet the person who received the call. It was Shubh's elder brother, Subhash. He gave her the address purely out of curiosity. That evening, Binny visited Shubh's house in Rajendra Nagar.

A servant opened the door and ushered her into Subhash's cabin. The latter was a High Court advocate and operated from his house.

'How may I help you, Mrs Bagga?' he said, after offering her tea.

'I'm an old friend of a friend of Aarisha's, Shubh's wife.'

'Who is this friend of Aarisha, if I may know please?'

'Vanav Thakur.'

'I don't think I've ever heard the name before.'

'You must have not, but I have a feeling . . .'

'Wait a minute. I think he was the one who called us from the US, the day Aarisha and Shubh met with the accident,' Subhash was charged up. His memory helped solve one of Binny's questions without her asking. So, Vanav was there when this accident happened and he was also the one who called both the families, Binny made a mental note.

'In fact, he was kind enough to send us their ashes,' Subhash said.

'What? The bodies were not seen by the families?' Binny couldn't suppress her shock.

Subhash said awkwardly, 'Actually it was costing us almost 35 lakhs to get the two bodies from the US. And that time, couple of decades back, we couldn't afford it.'

The fact that it costed that much money to get dead bodies from one country to another was news for Binny. She didn't have anything more to ask. After leaving Subhash, she called Vanav. A little chit-chat later, she asked, 'I was planning to visit the US with Anurag and Sirat. Can you guide me a bit? I've never been there before.'

'That's wonderful. You share the itinerary with me, and I'll let you know. Not that I've travelled there much. I'd only been there when I was studying medicine.'

'Oh, that's a long time ago. Aarisha was there in the US then, right?'

Vanav paused before replying, 'She was.'

'Okay. You guys must have met then, right?'

'No. I haven't met her since she got married,' Vanav said. The statement was part lie, part truth.

'Why not?'

'Just like that. We were never in each other's radar.'

'Never mind. I'll share the itinerary once Anurag prepares it. He's not good at these things.'

Binny's hunch was right. There was something wrong. Otherwise Vanav would have never lied to her.

9

The journey from Tosh to Triund where the other girls were and then eventually to Udaipur was emotionally claustrophobic for Aarisha. On the one hand, she had understood things about her boyfriend which she shouldn't have, or so she felt, and on the other, whenever he called she had to pretend that everything was alright. She had promised herself she wouldn't confront him till she had solid answers to her many questions.

A day after she reached her institute, he found Soni trying out different dresses in the room. Some of the dresses weren't even hers.

'When did you buy all this?' Aarisha asked.

'I borrowed them from a few of our batchmates.'

'Why? Anything coming up?'

'Kunal is coming here. It's a date,' Soni said with the kind of excitement which reminded her of the night when Vanav was about to come and she was getting ready in front of Pragya. The next instant, her eyes were moist. Aarisha excused herself and went inside the washroom. She cried looking at her reflection in the mirror. Her fairy tale romance had started showing nightmarish traits. She hadn't kissed a beast who turned into a prince. She'd kissed a prince who was slowly turning into a beast. She tugged at her panties and sat on the toilet to relieve herself while Googling 'how can we trace a person's location' on her phone. She went through the results meticulously till she reached a point in one of the articles. The article stated that if the person had a sim-based phone then his area, if not the exact location, could be traced via the network towers.

The moment Aarisha came out, she stopped short, looking at Soni. She had never seen her hypochondriac roommate look more beautiful. And she knew it more than just the makeup. When a woman is in love, there's a certain kind of glow in her visage and a gleam in her eyes. Aarisha went to Soni and said, 'I really hope you two make it.'

Soni understood why she said that.

'I hope whatever it is that's disturbing Vanav and your story, falls into place.'

'I hope so too,' Aarisha said, her voice lacking conviction. She went and sat on her bed with a frown.

'Now what's troubling you?' Soni asked.

'How can I get someone's phone records?'

'That someone is Vanav?' Soni looked at her incredulously. Aarisha's look made her forgo waiting for an answer. 'Didn't I ever tell you Kunal works in Vodafone?'

'What? Seriously? Why didn't you tell me before?' Aarisha was on her feet.

'I don't know why I didn't. Maybe there was no need to do so. And now you asked about phone records so ...' Soni shrugged.

'Can he do this for me?'

'Of course, he can, and he will. Wait, I'll speak to him when I meet him for dinner tonight.'

'Not tonight or not during the date. Don't spoil it. Ask him once you guys are done.'

'As you say.' Soni smiled.

Meanwhile, Binny lay awake on her bed after the daily grind scrolling through Facebook. Everything the Shergills and Subash had told her was going through her mind. She was making her own story. Vanav called them after their accident and yet he lied to her about the fact that he never met Aarisha. Why would he do so? And who was this girl who said her name was Aarisha Shergill too? On an impulse, Binny typed the name on her Facebook search bar and checked the results. She found the girl's profile in no time. She started going through everything—her pictures, her 'about me', her check-ins, etc. Vanav wasn't on any social media. Binny saw the Creator's Café pictures in Tosh as well. She tapped on her message button and then drafted a message.

Hi, I'm the one you met outside Vanav's house. Can we chat?

She sent the message. An hour later, a response came.

Hi, I remember you, Sumita. Chat about?

Vanav. Binny replied immediately.

Where are you stationed?

Delhi.

LET'S MEET TOMORROW?

YOU HERE?

NO, I'M IN UDAIPUR. BUT I CAN TRAVEL.

If someone was willing to travel from Udaipur to Delhi at the mere mention of a person's name, there had to be something important, Binny knew that.

Later that night, Soni messaged Aarisha.

WE DID IT. IT FELT SO GOOD AS HE FINALLY BEGAN TO CHANGE POSITIONS AS WELL.

HAPPY FOR YOU. Aarisha replied.

ALSO, I HAD A TALK WITH HIM. HE SAID HE WILL GIVE YOU THE RECORDS BUT DOESN'T WANT TO BE NAMED FOR THIS.

THAT'S FINE. LET ME SHARE THE NUMBER WITH YOU. YOU FORWARD IT TO HIM.

COOL.

The next day, when Aarisha was about to reach Delhi, Soni sent her the images of the phone records her boyfriend had dug out. They were of the past one year. As she started going through the records, her heart began to race, faster and faster. In the last one year, Vanav was more in Delhi and less in

237

Lucknow. When Pragya was in Delhi, so was he. Or at least his phone was. Pragya's last message to her echoed in her mind: *Do you know where your boyfriend is?* Does that mean she had seen Vanav or knew he was in Delhi? And did they meet? The questions were all legit but Aarisha was scared to answer them.

When she reached the café where Binny and she had fixed their meeting, she WhatsApped her:

I'M THERE IN THE CAFÉ. WHERE ARE YOU?

REACHING IN 5 MINS. DELHI TRAFFIC!

A reply came.

SURE, NO PROBLEM.

The messages immediately appeared on Vanav's phone. He knew the other number was Binny's. And he understood they were meeting in Delhi where he too was.

10

Binny found Aarisha sitting in a corner seat inside the café. They shook hands. Seeing her in daylight, unlike the last time, Aarisha realized she was a little older than she had thought. There was a slight awkwardness as Binny sat opposite her.

'Everyone calls me Binny,' she said.

Aarisha frowned slightly, trying to remember where she'd heard the name. And then it struck her that Vanav had showed her a photograph of his best friend.

'You are Vanav's best friend?'

'He is my first love as well,' Binny said.

Aarisha didn't know how to react.

'Sorry but he mentioned you to me only once, when I saw your photograph at his place.'

'That's why we are meeting, I guess. To know why Vanav did some things he shouldn't have.'

'What do you mean?'

'Do you know Aarisha Shergill?' Binny asked. A barista came. They both ordered iced tea.

'I'm Aarisha Shergill,' she said, giving Binny a what's-wrong-with-you look.

'Yeah, that I know. But you are from Tosh. I'm talking about Aarisha Shergill of Phagwara.'

Aarisha nodded. Binny decided it was better to hold back certain information till her understood what was going on.

'Are you guys in a relationship?'

'Yeah . . . for a few years now.'

'And Vanav has not told you about her?'

'No. Never.'

'Don't you think it's a weird coincidence that one man is in love with two women of different ages and with the same name?'

'This sounds weird, definitely.'

'Do you know Kathak?'

This was totally out of the blue but Aarisha found herself nodding.

Binny held her head in her hands. Oh God, I hope this isn't going the way I think it is, she thought and said aloud, 'Where are your parents? Tosh?'

'Yes. Why?'

'We need to meet them. As soon as possible,' Binny said.

The urgency in her voice scared Aarisha. It was obvious that Binny had cracked something which she hadn't.

'But I've got a kid and I won't be able to travel right away. Why don't you help me out with a few basic questions?'

'Questions like?'

'Their blood groups?'

'That I can ask them on the phone right now.'

'Please do.'

Binny saw Aarisha call someone and put the phone on speaker.

'Hello, papa, I just need to know your and mom's blood group.'

'Why, what happened suddenly?' The man on the speaker said.

'I need to fill in a form at the institute.'

'Oh, alright. My blood group is B+ while your mom's is O+.'

'Thanks, papa. I'll call you later.' Aarisha ended the call and looked up at Binny who was looking more tense than ever.

'What happened?'

'What's your blood group?' Binny asked.

'A+.'

The iced tea arrived. Neither touched it. Binny finished a glass of water though.

'Thanks to my frustration because of a late pregnancy, I've studied about these things in detail and know all this a little too well. This is technical but perhaps it'll help you understand what happened. Everyone has an ABO blood type and a Rh factor, positive or negative. And each of the biological parent donates one of the two ABO genes to their child. So, when an O gene is paired with an A gene, the child's blood type will be A. O is overridden in every case.'

Aarisha thought for a moment and said, 'So, if I'm my parents' child then ideally my blood group should be B+.'

Binny nodded and said, 'Not ideally. Technically. There's a difference.'

'But I have A+ group and it means . . .' Aarisha throat went dry before completing, 'I'm not their daughter.'

That's not the worst. The worst is that Vanav's blood group is A+, Binny thought but kept mum.

'You mentioned Aarisha Shergill of Phagwara. Who is she?'

'I'll tell you, but this is not the right time. I need to talk to Vanav once. But don't worry, she isn't a threat or anything,' Binny said conclusively. 'But tell me,' Binny said, 'how and where did you meet Vanav?' It was important for Binny to know their story first.

It had been an hour that Vanav had not moved an inch since he came and sat on the window couch at Samiha's place. He knew Binny and Aarisha were meeting somewhere in Delhi. And it wasn't rocket science to guess what they would be discussing. Samiha was busy making his sketch. She was waiting for him to speak. In the end, he did.

'Binny and Aarisha are meeting right now.'

Samiha's hands stopped working.

'What? How does Binny know her?'

'I don't know but she knows or how else would they have met.'

'Does Binny know about the truth?'

'Maybe she does, maybe she doesn't. But she can't know the whole truth. Only you and I know it.'

'Half-truths are always more dangerous,' Samiha said. A few minutes later, she said, 'You have to do something about it, captain.'

'If I don't do anything, I'll be the villain. And if I do anything I'll be more than a villain,' Vanav said. He excused himself to go to the washroom. Samiha saw his phone was lying on the couch. She went to it and picked it up for the first time. She had observed the pattern he made to unlock the phone and she did so in one second and memorized Binny's number from the contact list. If her captain had decided not to do anything, she would.

Aarisha finished telling Binny about all the anomalies that had happened in her life and about her rape.

'What do we do now?' Aarisha asked.

'Just go back. We need to know the truth first before charging anyone. I have to pick my daughter up from school now, so I'll have to leave. But let's be in touch. And don't talk to Vanav about our meeting or whatever we've discussed.'

'I won't.'

Binny stood up to leave when she got a call from an unknown number. She picked it up as she was stepping out of the café.

'Hello, is that Binny Bagga?' said a sweet female voice.

'Yes, who is this?'

'My name is Samiha. I'm Vanav's . . .' a pause later she said, 'friend and his girlfriend's mother. I think we should meet once.'

For a moment Binny thought she'd lost her voice.

11

Binny wanted to go to the address given to her by Samiha that day itself but family commitments crippled her intention. She could do nothing but wait for one more day before knowing what her first love was up to all these years.

Aarisha had gone to the station directly after meeting Binny. She had to catch the train to Udaipur. As she waited for her train, Aarisha grew restless. Whatever she had known had started to form a story in her mind and that story, according to her, was fast becoming her truth. If something wasn't adding up in that version of the truth it was her diary entries. For whatever was written in it was in direct contradiction to what she believed the truth was. And to address that one thing which wasn't adding up, she had to meet Vanav. Instead of a train to Udaipur, she booked a *tatkal* ticket for Lucknow. She boarded the train a few hours later and the next morning she was in Lucknow.

Vanav's phone on the side table, vibrated. He picked it up to see Ranisa's name flash. He answered the call.

'Hello, Ranisa.'

'Where are you?' Aarisha asked.

'Inside the command hospital,' Vanav lied.

'And I'm outside it. It's a surprise!' she said, pretending to sound jubilant.

Vanav took his time to speak, 'Why don't you go inside and speak to the receptionist? She'll take you to my cabin. I've a surgery, so I'll be with you in a few hours.' He ended the call and immediately called the reception and instructed them what to tell Aarisha.

Aarisha was duly escorted to Vanav's cabin.

Vanav quickly got dressed, instructing Samiha to book an air ticket on his phone from Delhi to Lucknow. It took him five hours to reach the command hospital in Lucknow. He changed into scrubs and entered his cabin.

'This is the first time that you've surprised me,' he said lowering his tall form into the swivel chair.

'I'm learning,' Aarisha smiled, trying to get her head around how someone could lie with such a straight face.

'Holidays in college?'

'Kind of. We've been given time off to figure out our internship. I thought I would do it in Lucknow so we can be together.'

'Of course.'

It was after dropping Sirat school that Binny went to the address given to her by the lady who claimed to be Aarisha's mother on phone. He remembered her name: Samiha. Though Binny was yet to share this information with Aarisha since she wanted to check first. Meeting Aarisha for the first time, she could sense she was the quintessential impulsive youngster who would do something and then think. Not the other way around.

When Samiha opened the door to Binny, the latter realized she was carrying a very different image of her in her mind. Binny thought Samiha would be someone who was slightly snobbish and restrained but the woman who opened the door carried a certain amicable aura about her. She looked like someone to whom you would tell your darkest secrets and she still won't mind.

As Binny settled on one of the bamboo chairs in the room, she asked, 'I'll be honest. I can't wait to know what you meant on the phone.'

'I said I'm her mother.'

'That I heard. But who is the father then? And how did you get my number?'

'Let me answer the second part first. I took your number from Vanav. He was here yesterday and till this morning. He doesn't know that I took your number or contacted you,' Samiha said as she sat opposite Binny. For a trice, the latter glanced at one of the sketches in the room and she immediately recognized Vanav.

'Are you two married?' Binny asked.

Samiha burst out laughing.

'No, we are the lucky ones. We aren't married. And honestly, Binny, I won't be able to explain what I mean to him and vice versa. Just understand that we prolonged our existence because of the other. Anyway, the important thing is that Vanav knows you met Aarisha.'

'He does? How?'

'I don't exactly know how, but yes he knows. He was upset but he wouldn't do anything about it because of his love for Aarisha.'

'Who is this Aarisha Shergill of Tosh?' Binny asked.

'The Aarisha Shergill of Pahgwara was his love. The one from Tosh is, you can say, his emotional experiment,' Samiha said. Binny looked on expectantly.

Aarisha and Vanav chatted desultorily about this and that in his cabin, after which Vanav took her out to lunch at the Renaissance Hotel and booked them into a room there as well. Just as she had expected, Vanav asked her to leave by eight that night.

At around ten, she called him. She slurred through the conversation and told Vanav that she was at Sky Bar and was unable to go to her room. He asked her to stay put and that he was on his way.

Vanav reached within the hour and found Aarisha alone in one of the corner tables of the pub, clearly very drunk. He paid the bill before lifting her in his arms and carrying her up to her room.

He deposited her on the bed and was about to drape the duvet over her when Aarisha tugged him close and started kissing him all over his face. He held her tight so she couldn't move.

'I won't let you go without you making love to me, Vanav,' she said groggily, gazing at him through half-open eyes that took an enormous effort to keep open.

'Yes, we will,' Vanav agreed and patiently waited for her to settle down and fall asleep.

'Make love to me Vanav, now!' she commanded and then passed out. Vanav straightened her out on the bed and gently patted her cheeks to check whether she was really asleep. She was.

Lying on her bed, Binny's head was reeling but she hadn't shared it with Anurag. She completed all the household duties for the day and retired to bed early. She still couldn't believe what Samiha had told her.

'Emotional experiment? What's that supposed to mean?' Binny had asked Samiha.

'Captain was there when Aarisha and Shubh died in the car accident. He was preparing to meet her after years but ended up seeing her dead body instead. He had been so sucked in by her, that seeing her dead he was sure there was nothing left in his life and thus he threw himself in front of a speeding car right in front of the hospital where the dead bodies initially were. When he came to consciousness, he realized that he wasn't hurt that badly. Since he was the one contacted first by the police officer from the accident site, captain introduced himself as family to the hospital authorities. He got the family phone numbers from Aarisha's phone and called both Aarisha's and Shubh's families in India. They wanted the bodies but because of some monetary issue it was decided that captain would do the last rites since they had no other person who could represent them and bring the ashes when he came to India.'

'And he did as asked?'

Samiha had nodded thoughtfully. 'Almost. He sent the ashes, but he didn't come.'

'Why?'

'That's because he learnt a certain thing which none of their friends or family knew except Aarisha and Shubh.'

'What was it?'

'Though I don't know the exact reason why they did it . . . Our guess was that they probably didn't want to have a baby that early. Shubh was a travel freak and probably thought a child would be a hindrance to his lifestyle. But that's strictly our guess.'

'What did they do?' Binny's patience was running out.

'Aarisha and Shubh had frozen their eggs and sperms respectively. Couples generally do it so that they can conceive later.'

That was the moment Binny started having a bad feeling about it all.

'Captain used his connections, manipulated documents and made sure he took over the frozen eggs and sperms.'

'What's Shubh's blood group?'

'A+ if I remember correctly, why?'

Binny was relieved to know what she had concluded earlier was incorrect. Vanav wasn't the younger Aarisha's father. Her parents were . . .

'So, this younger Aarisha is . . .' Binny began.

'Aarisha and Shubh's daughter.'

There was a long, contemplative silence. Then Binny spoke.

'Then why did you tell me you are the mother?'

'Captain needed a womb to get the baby delivered. I gave him my womb . . .' Samiha choked while saying the words. A pause later, she'd added, 'I shifted to the US for nine months with him. I used to ask him what if it is a boy? But there was this weird belief in his eyes when he told me it would be a girl. He had some indecipherable confidence that it would be a girl; a part of Aarisha. When we came back to India, we had little Aarisha with us. He went to Tosh with her, set up everything for her guardians who eventually acted like her parents, to her education, the café . . . He was blinded by his love for Aarisha, I could see it. I just didn't have the guts to question it.'

Binny gave her an incredulous look. The confession told Binny what the intensity of Samiha's relation must be with Vanav. Yes, they weren't married but she now knew she didn't need to malign their connection with the stamp of that man-made institution.

'Captain will be angry with me if he finds out that I've told you everything. It was a secret which I swore to keep but lately he's been different. I've never seen him like this before. He knows Aarisha has been digging around. Maybe she will one day start questioning him, but I know he will be quiet. He will take the hit for her. Captain told me a lot about you. And yesterday when I found out that you know about this Aarisha, I thought if there's one person who can be a bridge between captain and her, it's you. She won't ever understand what captain and I share. And she won't ever understand why I thought you would.'

'I do.' They looked into each other's eyes. Binny would never forget what she saw in the woman's eyes.

And now lying on her bed, Binny knew she had to call Aarisha in the morning and probably meet her during the weekend to explain to her that Vanav may have done things which were questionable but his intentions and love were beyond question.

It was late when Aarisha woke up with a start the next morning. She thought back to when she was still in the bar. The drinking was deliberate. The phone call to Vanav was also deliberate. She didn't have much faith in her acting skills, so she had to make it real. She swung her long legs out of the bed and stood up, ignoring her pounding head, and went over to the television in the room. She had kept the phone in a way where only the camera was popping out, capturing the on goings in the room. She picked her phone up and forwarded the recording to the point where Vanav carried her into the room. She saw him setting her down on the bed and herself trying to drunkenly initiate a grand seduction; him holding her firm without giving her any room to manoeuvre until she eventually gave up and fell asleep in his embrace; him gently covering her with a duvet. The next part was intriguing: he seemed to be searching for something and then stopped when he had apparently found it. The video did not allow Aarisha to see what it was until he turned around with her diary in his hands. He sat and wrote for some time and then carefully returned the diary to where he had found it.

Aarisha stopped the video and fetched the diary. She opened the page to the most recent diary entry:

Dear Diary

After a long time, he made love to me. Until the wee hours. We were exhausted by the end of it. I can't explain how it feels when he cuddles me. I hope such moments happen more and more. I'm sleepy now. I will write to you later.

Aarisha sank to the floor as her knees buckled. The words in the diary were not hers. Neither were the sentiments expressed in it. But the worst of it was that it was all in her own handwriting. Her entire life had been a manipulation! Aarisha furiously ripped out the pages of the diary, one by one. Sobbing brokenly, she flung them into the air like confetti.

Hours later, Vanav called. She didn't answer her phone. He continued calling at short intervals, but there was no response from her at all. She sat on the floor like she had been carved from stone. Vanav swiped the key card to the room and found her on the floor by the low table. He could tell that something was terribly wrong.

'What happened, Ranisa?' he ran to her and knelt.

'Stay away from me,' Aarisha whispered, her voice throaty and low, almost a growl.

12

'You're the one who raped me, isn't that right?' Aarisha looked him in the eye, her beautiful eyes narrowing. 'The man who can kill the guys who only touched me, who can kill my best friend only because she knew you were in Delhi and Lucknow as you told me, but that same man does nothing about the fact when I'd been found raped? You really thought you would slip away with that?'

'Ranisa . . .'

'Will you stop with this "Ranisa" shit? This respect, this care, this concern . . . all pure bullshit!'

'Please don't jump to wild conclusions without knowing the truth,' Vanav said gently.

'The truth?' she scoffed. 'What could this wonderful truth be, huh? That it leads someone to rape a girl and then alter her memory in such a way that she starts believing that she was in love, *in love*, with her rapist? Tell me, can there be any bigger truth than that? And all this because you love her? Love? Really? What a shame you turned out to be Vanav? The man who talks about love so highly, is nothing but a victim of lust and obsession.'

Vanav sat back on the floor, looking like he had been bludgeoned. The dream that he had carefully fabricated, crumbled before his eyes like a sandcastle. His years of preparation, secrecy and sacrifice—all of it coming to nothing. And above all her misinterpretation of it all.

Aarisha stood up and paced the room, her hands on her hips and eyes bloodshot.

'What a plan I must say. First rape her, then copy her handwriting and fill up a diary, give her memory altering medicines and then convince her that she's always been in love with you. Why? Because you have been obsessing about her so much that you didn't mind crossing any lines. Be it exposing her to a traumatic experience like rape . . .'

'I didn't rape you, Ranisa,' Vanav said softly.

'You did. Both physically and emotionally. Why else would you report it to the police that I was raped? You are my emotional rapist as well. In fact, now I know why you didn't react much when Deep tried to molest me. That's because you'd already savoured my body. It didn't matter much to you, right? And tell you what? I met your friend Binny and found out that my parents are also not real. I'm not the daughter of those two who claim to have raised me. Or is it that you have killed my biological parents as well? Have you Vanav? Please answer me,' Aarisha's pitch had risen to a deafening level by the time she finished.

Vanav remained quiet. He couldn't tell her who her real parents were.

'So, your silence confirms it. You have turned me into a fucking guinea pig. I don't remember anything except for things which you want me to remember or know half of which are lies. White lies. How could you do this to me,

Vanav? What did I do to deserve this? Only because you were obsessed with me? Only because you wanted to fuck me?'

'Ranisa!' Vanav hollered and then said gently, looking at the floor, 'Let *me* tell you the truth . . . Am I allowed to speak?'

'Of course, you can, but I won't believe anything you say. You've been toying with my trust for years now. You think I'll ever believe anything you do or say? You have killed my parents. You are so heartless that you don't think twice before saying that even your parents are dead whereas the truth is that they alive and kicking. What will they think of you if they find out about this? I'm never going to forgive you ever, Vanav Thakur. And if you have any shame left in you, you'll leave me the fuck alone. I don't want to see your face ever again, d'you understand? You don't love me. You've never loved me. You can never, ever, love. Not me or anyone. All I was to you, was a lusty obsession. A cheap emotional experiment.'

A tear fell from Vanav's eye to the floor.

'I'm checking out and leaving for Udaipur. Don't you dare follow me. Do not try to stop me. I don't want you in my life anymore. But yes, before I leave, I'm filing a FIR here against you, my fucking rapist. People like you should rot in prison. A shame for the Army, a shame for men, a shame for everything and everyone you ever stood for.' Aarisha picked up her bag and stormed out of the room.

Vanav was frozen to his spot. Sometime later, he received a call from the local police station telling him that a report had been filed against him for raping a young girl a couple of years back.

'I'm guilty as charged,' Vanav said, telling them he was in his command hospital hostel and they could come and arrest him.

Ending the call, Vanav slowly dragged himself upright and trudged out of the room defeated. He went to the staff quarters in the hospital.

You don't love me. You've never loved me. You can never, ever, love. Not me or anyone.

Vanav took a long bath with the words cutting him like blades. He dried himself, donned his uniform. He called his mother, listened to her but didn't say anything. Then he called his father, heard him speak but didn't say anything either. He switched his phone off and connected to the hostel Wi-Fi. He opened Samiha's WhatsApp window and started recording a voice note:

So, it happened. She understood that all of it was a plan but unfortunately, she didn't understand that love was the only motive. I don't know where to begin. Where did it begin? From the time I saw her in my room in bridal wear? Maybe.

From that moment till today, never has a moment passed when she hasn't been in my conscious mind. She has raised a storm of questions in me all these years. And answering them, I grew from a boy to a man. Not that I got the answers to every question, but I sought them doggedly nevertheless. In the questions, I discovered life's limitations, while in my quest for the answers I found my own liberation.

Everyone has an edge. And if you are afraid of bleeding because of that edge in the other person, then you can't claim to have loved the person. At first, I thought Aarisha's edge was her indifference towards me. She ignored me knowing I loved her. You know, I always wondered if it would damage her if she was in touch with me? I wasn't even asking her to be in a relationship. Just a hi-hello from time to time. Didn't matter how much I craved and died for just one message from her, for just seeing her, even if it meant from a distance. To draw her inside my reality bubble. And the more she was indifferent towards me, the more I grew desperate. That's when I started giving myself pain to keep her alive within me. Somewhere, I felt connected with her by doing so. I can never forget the way she held my hand in the train while Papa and I were going to drop her at her place in Phagwara. Her nails dug into my flesh and her tears had dried on me. That was the first time I felt that she belonged to me. And yet I couldn't understand why she ignored me when Papa and I were taking leave from her house. I wasn't Daksh bhaiya. If she had chosen me, I would have fought everyone for her. Every-fucking-one. I would have never betrayed her. I would have never left her alone to fight any battle. But the reward I was given for loving someone genuinely was loneliness and a truck load of what-ifs. My life became my imagination. I was forever imagining myself with her in everyday situations. I dated her, I married her, I made love to her, I made happy moments with her, but all of it was in my imagination. And then one day she unfriended me from Yahoo Messenger. That's when I realized that I meant nothing to her. To move on from someone, one needs to hold onto someone else. But she was my everything. I didn't need anyone else. To be honest, I was sick and tired of being a nobody to her. I wanted to be somebody. Somebody who had some space in her life. And I thought it was done . . . her tattoo told me that. If she never loved or cared for me, if I was actually a nobody to her, she wouldn't have tattoo RANISA on her nape. It was a name I had given her. And that tattoo was her silent rebellion. And just when I thought I would have some space in her life, death took her away. Just like that. I clearly remember her body. Bruised and battered. And I could do nothing about it. Till I learnt that her eggs and Shubh's sperm were frozen. That was my last chance to hold onto something which was her. A part of her. That was enough for me to give life another chance. Aarisha for me was God. My love for her was my temple. When destiny broke my God's idol, I made another idol out of a piece of the original. This time I thought my love would win because I planned for it, I worked for it, I did everything I could to make it work. The only thing I forgot was you can't force-fit anything against nature. The latter has its own way of defeating you in the most mocking manner possible.

People will say Aarisha was my first love and that's why I was so fixated by her. But she was my only. People always assume that there will be many more in life. But with me there was no possibility of anyone else. That's why I named her daughter Aarisha Shergill. Not anything else. For me her daughter was her. But guess what? It was all a big illusion. I feel like I've suddenly woken up from a long sleep. The greatest thing I learnt from Ranisa was the power of silence. It conquers time as well.

I thought of telling her the truth. I thought of telling her about my love but then I realized she won't believe anything I say. But just because she won't believe it, the truth won't change. I always loved Aarisha. I always will. Also, it's high time I accept all of it was a mistake. A mistake by a man who was soul-deep in love with a woman but also so blinded by it that he chose to forgo commonsense to keep something alive which was never meant to be.

Aarisha's ashes are there in my locker. I never sent the real ashes to her family. I visit the ashes every day. That's my shrine. You have all my passwords. Get it out and give it to her daughter. She deserves to know *this. But not from me. Also, if the police come looking for her parents in Tosh, tell the police it's all me, not them. So, spare them. I know you love me but I'm a cursed soul, someone who neither got the love he craved nor gave the love you and Binny expected from him. I'm indebted to both of you. I shall pay you back in some other life. I promise. This one was for Aarisha. This was for Ranisa. I made the mistake of giving life a chance after Ranisa's death. I won't repeat it.*

Vanav sent the voice note. And deleted the Wi-Fi connection. Aarisha's words still echoed within him.

You don't love me. You've never loved me. You can never, ever, love. Not me or anyone.

He reached into the drawer in his bedside table and extracted his service revolver. He sat placing the revolver at his temple and said, 'I think I should have done this a long time ago, but I was greedy to live a little longer with you. A part of you, if not the entire you. I love you, Ranisa. Maybe not the way the world knows love, but the way you made me experience love.'

There was a knock on the door. It was the police. Vanav shut his eyes tight and pulled the trigger.

Epilogue I

BINNY

It's early in the morning. She is standing in the bathroom attached to her bedroom. Taking a morning bath and coming out of the bathroom ready to take on the household chores is something Binny has done everyday of her life. But today is different. She doesn't have any energy to do anything. Not even to breathe. She cried all of last night. Not only has she lost her best friend and first love, she's lost someone who remained within her. And that pain simmers in the soul as long as one is alive.

There's a knock on the door. Binny opens it. Sirat is standing outside. She looks at her mother as if there's something wrong with her.

'Mumma, you haven't put the red dot today,' Sirat says, implying the vermillion.

Binny kneels and creasing her daughter's head, she says, 'Today is an exception. I won't wear it today. From tomorrow your mumma will be back.'

'You mean it's your cheat day?'

Binny kisses her forehead, holds her tightly in her arms and nods, saying, 'Yes, it's my cheat day.'

Epilogue II

SAMIHA

Samiha has been sketching non-stop for the last fifteen hours. Her sketches have never been this detailed. It is something straight out of her memory—when she was carrying Aarisha in her. Till then, Vanav and she had connected only to heal each other in their own twisted way. But she saw that he truly cared for her, and the respect he showered her with during those nine months made her fall for him. She knew he could never be hers, but she was happy because she chose to be his. He'd made her feel like a mother. He had made her feel she was worth someone's care and attention. He had made her feel beautiful within. It wasn't only her womb that she had surrendered to him but her heart and soul as well. She knows that she too must experience Vanav's heartache of living a life without Aarisha. She will have to live considering his absence as his permanent presence around her, within her.

Once she is done with her sketch, she simply holds the canvas and weeps. *I love you, captain, I love you so much.* She keeps mumbling under her urgent breath. As she rubs her face on the sketch, her tears become his.

Epilogue III

AARISHA

O *ne day I want to swim with you naked in this river.*
Aarisha's own words—the ones she's told Vanav—echo in her mind. She is sitting by the Tosh river with two urns beside her, each covered with fine linen crimson cloth, stretched taut over the mouths and secured with black string around the neck to keep its contents from spilling out. The river is quiet, just like her. She takes a deep breath and stares at the two urns—one contains the ashes of her mother whom she has never met. She has only seen her in the form of ashes. The other urn contains Vanav's ashes. Vanav was someone who loved her mother so much that his love overflowed and inundated *her*, the daughter of the woman he loved. *Aarisha, for me, was God. My love for her was my temple. When destiny broke my God's idol, I made another idol out of a piece of the original. Was I wrong?* Vanav's words ricochet in her mind.

Binny had taken her to Samiha; the woman whose womb she had been born from. Binny arranged for the photographs of her parents. She was their part but she didn't know them at all.

Samiha had sent her the voice note which Vanav had sent her before shooting himself. The guilt hangs heavy inside her. If only she had waited one more day . . . Binny would have called her and told her the whole truth. Perhaps then she wouldn't have seen him as an emotional rapist but rather a consequence of a badly broken heart. Had she waited, this catastrophe could have been averted.

Aarisha takes the urns, one at a time, in her hands and kisses them. She presses them against her head and then stands up. She slowly strips herself and then smears all the ash from both urns on her naked body. She remembers what Vanav had once told her.

You know this thing we call love, it's like a dense forest. As you enter, you hear the growl of several wild beasts. At times, you may even encounter them. Insecurity is the most ferocious beast in this jungle. Whether to fall victim or vanquish it to continue one's quest to unearth the greatest treasure ever, which is also hidden in this very forest, is the lover's call.

Her only redemption is, she thinks, if she can one day understand Vanav's love for her mother. Perhaps then she will understand his madness for her as well. A man spent his entire life just being in love with a woman. A woman he could never touch, never hear or talk to. A woman who spent a life blanketing her love for the man with silence because she had duties to fulfil. She suddenly feels very tiny and insignificant compared to her mother and Vanav.

Standing all ash-smeared by the river, Aarisha takes a deep breath, and then plunges into the river, swimming strongly in the freezing currents of the water as the ash is washed from her body and becomes one with the water.

I've taken mine. What's your call, Ranisa?

Acknowledgments

Thank you, Milee Ashwarya, for being a guardian angel and allowing me and my stories to breathe out to the public each time. The journey becomes sheer joy when there's someone like you guiding me. To many more, cheers!

My gratitude to the marketing and sales team of Penguin Random House India for lending their prompt support to my books whenever needed.

Thanks to all my friends for punctuating me whenever needed.

Thanks, Trisha, for the smooth edits.

Tight hugs to my family for allowing me to be myself.

Thank you to each one of my readers for appreciating my work time and time again. I am deeply indebted for the love and support you all show me.

Ranisa—thank you, for if not for you, I wouldn't have known the meaning of my inner ruins. Every moment with you is a life education. And if I write any more about this, people will misinterpret it.

R—thank you for being the reason for me to be a better human being each day. And, the reason for a fatalist like me to connect to the survivor within.